For The Love Of Pete

To
Sherry

Maxwell
West

For The Love Of Pete

A Romantic Mystery

J Maxwell West

Copyright in 2012 by J Maxwell West

ISBN: 13: 978-1479262090

10: 1478262099

All rights reserved. No part of this book may be reproduced or transmitted in any form or by any means, electronic or mechanical, including photocopying, recording, or by any information storage and retrieval system, without permission in writing from the Copyright owner.

This is a work of fiction. Names, characters, places and incidents either are the product of the author's imagination or are used fictitiously, and any resemblance to any actual persons, living or dead, events or locales is entirely coincidental.

This book was printed by CreateSpace in the United States of America.

To order additional copies of this book, contact:

jpbooks.net
1-870-578-7858
west4937@sbcglobal.net

Dedication

This book is dedicated to the members of my family who have meant so much to me.

Of special importance are my mom and dad. Dad was killed in a car accident when I was sixteen, and mom passed away in 1996. Mom actually lived and raised four children in Stan and Pat Dover's house on Parkview in Jonesboro, Arkansas.

Then are my siblings, two brothers and a sister who allowed me to mistreat them as we grew up.

Most important in my life, now are my wife, Polly, and our children. We enjoy three girls and two boys who have given us five grandchildren and four great-grandchildren.

I also have to include my wife's mom and dad who celebrated their 72nd wedding anniversary this past May.

I have always had a strong sense of family and you will find it revealed in this "For the Love of" trilogy.

The people who proofed this book are also included in this dedication page. Their untiring effort meant so much to the quality of this book.

Memphis, TN
The Shooting
June 10

    The shooter was sitting in the driver's seat of the 2004 dark gray Mercury Grand Marquis waiting for Peter Clyde Dover and Janie Albert. Pete was an attorney working for the Department of Justice and Janie worked for the law firm of Sneed, Weeks and King. Pete and Janie had been to Playhouse on the Square's production of "August: Osage County". Checking her watch, the shooter saw it was 11:00 p.m. Her contact told her Pete drove a 2011 blue Ford Taurus with Tennessee tags, number CDF 241 and that the play would be over at 11:15 p.m. She had arrived at the Playhouse on the Square parking lot early. It had been no trouble to locate Pete's car and she was lucky enough to find a parking place directly in front of the Taurus. "It can't be much longer," she thought, as she checked her 45 caliber ACP that had a noise suppresser.
    From where the shooter was parked, she could see the exit door to the Playhouse and she noticed people were beginning to come out. Nervously, she checked her weapon again. She needed to calm down so she began to practice the most effective technique she had learned to slow her heart rate.

She began to concentrate on a relaxing image. This time she was sunbathing on the beach in Maui. In no time at all her heart rate was down to 69 beats per minutes. "Perfect," she thought.

Several of the cars were leaving as the shooter saw the couple that she expected to be Pete Dover and his date. Janie appeared to be in her late twenties. She wore a black, low cut dress with spaghetti straps. Her hair was an attractive, long, dish-water blond. Her three inch heels made her look as tall as Pete. Pete looked very "lawyerly" in his dark gray suit with a white shirt and red tie.

Just as Pete started to open the door for his date, the shooter opened her door and yelled, "Pete". Pete looked back at her and she fired her 45 ACP. It was a good shot and Pete went down. Next, she turned her attention to Pete's date. His date was screaming and beginning to run when she was shot twice in the center of the back and fell face forward.

Even with a silencer on her weapon, people were beginning to gather around the two people on the ground. One woman was calling 911. There happened to be a doctor in the crowd and he was checking on the condition of the couple. A big burley looking man with a dark beard was getting the license number of the 2005 Mercury Grand Marquis as it burned rubber leaving the parking lot.

+++++

The shooter pulled the Mercury into a Wal-Mart parking lot which was ten miles from the Playhouse on the Square. She pulled the Mercury up beside a 2012 silver Lexus LX SUV. Getting out of the Mercury, she made sure she had everything in her bag. The Mercury was clean. It was as though she had never been in it. As she opened the door to the Lexus, she took off the gloves she had been wearing to make sure she left no prints in the Mercury. With a little luck she would be back home in Atlanta in time for breakfast.

+++++

From the identification in her purse, the Memphis Police discovered that the woman on the ground was Janie Albert. The two slugs in her back had done their job. Janie was pronounced dead by the EMTs without transporting her to the hospital. It was now left to the police to notify her family. According to the information in her purse, her parents lived in Jackson, Mississippi. A call was made to the Jackson police to ask them to notify Mr. and Mrs. Carl Albert who lived at 1972 Live Oak.

In the meantime, the doctor and EMTs were working with the man on the ground. He was still alive. When the police turned their attention to him they found they knew him. Having been in court with Pete Dover, they knew he was a lawyer for the Justice Department working in Shelby County. They also knew that his family owned the Dover Detective Agency. Calling headquarters, they told the dispatcher about the death of Janie Albert and the action they had taken. Then they shared what they knew about Pete Dover and asked the dispatcher to contact his family and tell them he was being taken to Baptist East in critical condition.

Other officers on the scene had been questioning the people who were still left in the parking lot. No one had seen the shooter, however, several had seen the dark gray 2005 Mercury Grand Marquis and at least two had given them the license number. It had Texas tags, number 886 TWC. An APB had already been put out for the car. Two of the officers continued to question people at the scene, as well as, the owners of the Playhouse. Two other officers went to Baptist East Hospital to check on Dover and talk to his family.

+++++

Andy and Sue Dover, Pete's parents, were in the waiting area of the emergency room when the two officers arrived. The officers introduced themselves to the Dovers as Officer Dick Goodman and Officer Joe Dugan. They asked if they had heard anything concerning Pete's condition.

Andy said, "We just got here and talked with a nurse who told us that the doctors were still working with Pete. She also said she didn't know how long it would be before the doctor talked to them about Pete's condition. That's all we have been able to find out. Please tell us what you know."

"We know he is in critical condition. There was a doctor at the scene. If he had not been there Pete may not have made it to the hospital. I believe the doctor rode in the ambulance with him to the hospital," replied Goodman.

"That's what we understand," said Andy. "What happened? When they called us, all they said was that Pete had been shot and we needed to go to Baptist East. That's all we know."

Dugan responded, "The best we can figure, someone in a dark gray Mercury was waiting for Pete and/or his date to come out of the Playhouse. It seems their cars were parked nose to nose and when Pete started to open the door for his date, he was shot once in the chest. As he was going down, his date turned and started to run. That's when she was shot twice in the back."

"Who is she and what is her condition?"

"I'm sorry; I took it for granted that you knew. The woman's name was Janie Albert and she was pronounced dead at the scene." Dugan continued, "While we're waiting, we really need to ask you a couple of questions."

Both Sue and Andy agreed to try to answer any questions the officers might have.

"Did you know Janie Albert?" asked Dugan.

"We know—we knew her. Pete had worked with her when he was at Sneed, Weeks and King. I believe she was a paralegal there. We also knew they were dating. However, Pete had told us they were simply good friends." replied Sue.

"Do you know why anyone would want to kill her?" asked Goodman.

"I don't have any idea," said Andy. "Sue and I know nothing of her business or personal life except that she was a friend of Pete."

"What about Pete, do you know why anyone would want to kill him?" continued Goodman.

"It must be related to his job. Maybe he has a case that he is working on that is dangerous. However, if he does, he hasn't talked to us about it."

Sue interrupted, "I asked Pete not to take that job. I was afraid something like this might happen, but, he wanted to do it. He told me he would be alright and besides he said he could get run over crossing the street. He has to be okay." With tears in her eyes, Sue turned her back to the officers and walked to the women's restroom. Once Sue got her emotions under control, she decided to call Gracie before she came out of the restroom.

Gracie was Stan and Pat Dover's middle child and only daughter. She was Sue's sister-in-law. However, since they worked together in the Dover Detective Agency they had become more like sisters. Sue had been there for Gracie when Susan, Gracie's daughter, had been kidnapped. Now Sue needed Gracie to be there for her.

When Gracie answered her phone it was around 1:00 a.m., so she knew immediately that something was wrong. "Sue, what's going on?"

Sue told her that she and Andy were at the Baptist East Hospital and that Pete had been shot. He was in critical condition. Sue also said, "Gracie, I need you."

"I'll be there in twenty minutes," replied Gracie as she hung up the phone.

By then, Sanders, Gracie's husband and the lead detective for the agency, was awake and wondering what all the commotion was about.

"Pete's been shot and he is critical. He's at Baptist East. Andy and Sue need us now. Get it in gear, I told Sue we would be there in twenty minutes."

+++++

Eighteen minutes later Gracie and Sanders were almost running into the emergency room waiting area. Sue saw them and ran to them. Gracie held Sue for a very long time as Andy told Sanders what was happening. "All we really know is that Pete and his date were shot coming out of the Playhouse on the Square. His date, Janie Albert, was killed and Pete is critical. They have been in there with him for over two hours trying to save his life."

"Let's walk," said Sanders. "Need some coffee." Sanders had always been someone to use as few words as possible.

As the two men walked down the hall, Andy filled Sanders in on other things the officers had told him. Sanders had retired from the FBI to come to work for the Dover Detective Agency about four years ago. He was a no nonsense kind of guy and a very good detective. He taught all the Dover's everything he had learned with the FBI. In four short years, the Agency had become one of the leading detective agencies in Memphis. Sanders had been married to Andy's sister, Gracie, for four years.

When the men came back they were carrying coffee, chips, and sweet rolls. Sue and Gracie had found a table and the men had joined them. Looking at his watch, Andy said, "Its 2:45 and we haven't heard anything from a doctor. I need to hear something."

At that very moment, two men, who looked like they could be the doctors, came through the double doors and headed for their table. The older one looked to be about Sanders' age and appeared totally wiped out. The other looked more like a college student. The older man introduced himself as Doctor James Caan and told the group that he had been at the Playhouse when Pete was shot. Doctor Caan then introduced Doctor Lester Miller as the surgeon.

Andy hurriedly introduced himself and the rest of the family. "My concern is my son, how is he?"

"He is one lucky young man," said Doctor Miller. "Doctor Caan was able to keep him alive until we could operate on him. The bullet went completely through his chest. There was a lot of bleeding and there were several things we had to put back together but we have every reason to believe he will fully recover. He is still unconscious but his vitals are good. Hopefully, he will be awake in a few hours."

"Can we see him?" asked Sue.

"As I said, he is unconscious. However, if you would like to see him, I will have a nurse come get you as soon as they get him set up in ICU."

"That would be perfect, thank you," said Sue.

As the doctors were leaving, the two police officers stopped them and were told they might be able to see Pete tomorrow afternoon. The police would need to check with the nurse to find out how he is doing.

+++++

The 2011 silver Lexus LX SUV pulled off the highway for a "pit stop" just outside of Birmingham, AL. The woman who got out was no more than five feet tall and may not have weighed one hundred pounds. She had dark hair, was dressed in a dark blue pants suit with dark heels and couldn't have been over thirty years old. Looking at her, no one would ever believe she had shot two individuals just a few hours before.

While the woman was in the convenience store, her cell phone rang. Answering it, she heard the caller say, "According to my information, Janie Albert is dead but Peter Dover is still alive. I'll get back to you." With that the caller hung up.

"Damn, shit. I could have sworn that was a deadly shot," she said to herself.

Chapter Two

Memphis, TN
The Investigation Begins
June 11

    It was 7:00 a.m. and the officers involved with the Dover shooting were meeting with the detectives at police headquarters. Information about the shooting was coming in slow. They knew the shooter was driving a dark gray Mercury. However, it seemed no one had seen the shooter. They had found three 45 caliber shell casings they believed had come from the shooter's weapon. Around 4:00 a.m., they had received a call concerning a dark gray Mercury on the parking lot of Wal-Mart. After investigation, they discovered it was the car used in the shooting. The lab boys were giving it a good going over. The Mercury was stolen with junk yard tags on it.
    The Wal-Mart employee who called it in said he saw a woman get out of the Mercury and into a "new looking" silver Lexus. He did not get the license number. The woman was small, young and very good looking which was probably why he noticed the car exchange. Once he heard the APB on the radio, he called the police.
    After Detectives Jerry Searcy and Mark Melton were assigned to work the case, Searcy asked, "What do I do about the Dover Detective Agency."

"What do you mean?" asked the Captain Davis.

"I mean, they are going to be looking over my shoulder every inch of the way. Can I tell them to "bug off" and let the police handle the case?"

Captain Davis replied, "There is not much we can do about their involvement. Anyway, I have always found Sanders to be a good detective and very helpful in any cases we happened to be working together---after all he was with the FBI for almost forty years. It might be that he could teach the two of you a few things."

+++++

By 7:30 a.m., the people who make up the Dover Detective Agency were meeting. Andy was leading the meeting. Sam, the youngest of the Dover kids, was there along with Sanders and, of course, Stan Dover the father of the clan. Stan had been 70 years old when he had won the Power Ball Lottery of 145 million dollars. Now he was 75.

Looking back, Stan decided that was when the Dover family had become the "Dover Clan". When anything happened to one of them, the whole family came together to fix the problem. It had been that way when people were trying to kill Stan about five years ago. It had been that way when Susan, Gracie's daughter, had been kidnapped about three years ago. Now that Pete, Andy and Sue's son, was in trouble, the whole clan was here to help. Whoever tried to kill Pete had no idea what he or she was up against. Sue, Gracie, and Pat (Stan's wife and Pete's grandmother) were still at the hospital with Pete.

"While Sam is busy with the Casidy case, the rest of us will give all our attention to finding out who tried to kill Pete," said Andy. "Sanders, where do we start?"

"First, we try to determine who the shooter wanted to kill. It could have been Janie Albert. She could have been working on a case that included some dangerous individuals. Stan, maybe you could meet with Sneed, Weeks and King and see what you can learn."

Stan replied, "I'll be glad to check out Janie Albert's work life. It might be wise for me to also see what I can find out about her personal life. Her funeral will probably be tomorrow. I'll be glad to represent the family at her service."

"That all sounds good to me," said Sanders. "Andy could you check out the US Attorney's Office. Nose around; see if you can find out if they are prosecuting anyone who might try to kill Pete. I'll see if I can find out anything at the police department. I have worked with Captain Davis and feel he will try to help us."

The phone was ringing and since Sue was at the hospital, Andy answered it. Everyone expected it to be the hospital so they looked at Andy, trying to read Andy's face. His smile said it all. Then they heard him say, "I'll be right there."

"Pete is awake and he is talking. Let's all go see what we can learn. We're finished here for the moment. You have your assignments." With that, Andy hurriedly left the office.

Since everyone was going in different directions after they left the hospital, they all went in separate cars. However, before Sanders could get away, the phone rang again. The caller ID identified the caller as Memphis Police. The caller identified himself as Detective Jerry Searcy. Searcy said, "Sanders, can we get together today?"

Sanders looked at his watch and said, "How about meeting you at my office at 11:00 a.m."

"Sounds good to me. I'll see you then," Searcy said as he hung up the phone.

+++++

The nurse in ICU, who was taking care of Pete, was only letting two people at a time go in and see him. Sue and Andy were in ICU with him, but as Andy came out, the others began to take turns, except Sue. She would not leave Pete's bedside. Sanders was the last to get a turn before the visiting hour was over. As Sanders started to leave, Pete said, "Sanders, if I had to guess I would say this shooting has something to do with Sneed, Weeks, and King. All the time I worked there, I had the feeling that something was going on. Janie called me a couple of days ago very upset. She wouldn't tell me what was wrong over the phone. She said we needed to meet which is why we went to the Playhouse in the first place."

Sanders started to ask a question when the nurse came in and said everyone had to leave, visiting hours were over. As Sue and Sanders walked back toward the ICU waiting area, Sue said, "Sanders, what Pete said to you was the first time he would even talk about the shooting. No one else could get him to say anything about it. He just kept assuring them that he was alright and he wanted someone to talk to Mr. and Mrs. Carl Albert."

Sanders said, "We've assigned that to Stan. I believe he plans to go to the funeral."

+++++

The other members of the family were waiting for Sue and Sanders. Sanders shared what Pete had told him about the shooting and said he had to leave. He told them he was meeting Detective Searcy at the office at 11:00 a.m.

Gracie said, "Sue and I plan to go home for a bath and a change of clothes. Mom said she would stay at the hospital. I think Sam's wife, Daisy, is coming up to sit with her. Sanders, check with me after your meeting with Searcy, maybe we can have lunch."

+++++

Stan went to Sneed, Weeks and King Law Firm included the entire, very nice, office building at 1344 Winchester. It was just off I-240 in East Memphis. They had one hundred ten lawyers and one hundred fifty support staff working for them. As Stan walked toward the receptionist desk, he could smell "old money". Everything was new and very expensive. He didn't have an appointment and knew he may not get in to see any of the partners. However, when he told the receptionist who he was and that he would like to see one of the partners, she picked up her phone and called Mr. Donald Weeks.

She said, "Mr. Weeks will be right out. Have a seat."

It was less than five minutes when a large man dressed in a dark gray suit came to the receptionist's desk. She said, "Mr. Dover, this is Mr. Donald Weeks and he will see you now."

As Stan stood, Weeks invited Stan to follow him back to his office. They passed three large offices. Stan noticed that each one had a large window and was furnished with expensive looking furniture. The smell of "old money" became stronger as they walked. Once in Weeks' office, Weeks invited Stan to sit down and said, "As you might expect, we are pretty torn up here today. Janie Albert was one of our most valued employees. I don't know what we will do without her."

"Do you have any ideas why anyone would want to kill her?" asked Stan.

"No. But I assumed someone was trying to kill Pete and she just happened to be there. Do you believe she was the target?"

"We don't know. Was she working on anything that would cause someone to want her dead?"

"Not that I know of, but most of her work was research for Bob Wilkins. He isn't here today. You might make an appointment with him through the receptionist out front."

Stan felt a little "put off" so he asked, "What about Pete? Do you know anyone who would want to kill him?"

"No I don't. He only worked for us about a year. I never really got a chance to know him. How is his condition today?"

That same feeling of distance was there for Stan, but he answered, "Pete was conscious this morning and the doctors say he will make it."

"I'm glad for that," said Weeks. Then he stood as a signal for Stan to know he was being dismissed.

Stan stopped at the receptionist's desk on the way out. He made an appointment to see Bob Wilkins. As he walked to his car, he couldn't shake the feeling that all was not right with Sneed, Weeks and King.

Back at his office, Stan called Mr. and Mrs. Carl Albert in Jackson, MS to offer words of condolences, as well as, find out the funeral service arrangements for their daughter, Janie.

+++++

Andy was at the US Attorney's Office cooling his heels waiting to see the US Attorney. Pete had introduced her to Andy at some kind of social gathering. Pete had told him that she was a hard nosed prosecutor who didn't take anything from anybody. However, Andy had sized her up as one of those people who got a little power and wanted everybody to know it. This was confirmed today when she keep him waiting for over thirty minutes even though he had an appointment.

Breaking though his thoughts, Andy heard Debra Witcher, the US Attorney, say, "Sorry to have kept you waiting, come on back to my office." Witcher was dressed in a brown business suit with a white blouse. Her hair was short and light brown; she was about 5'8" tall and probably weighed 170 pounds which was mainly muscle. Her appearance suggested she would be at home on the football field. Witcher's office was very masculine and suggested power.

"How is Pete this morning?" asked Witcher.

"He is better, he is awake and alert. We have every reason to believe he will have a full recovery."

"What can I do for you this morning?"

Andy responded, "We're trying to find the person or persons responsible for killing Janie and trying to kill Pete. I wanted to start with his case load here."

"Then you don't believe it was just a random shooting?"

"No, we feel sure it was someone trying to kill Pete or Janie. They succeeded in killing Janie. At this point, we are not sure which one they were after. Janie worked with Bob Wilkins of Sneed, Weeks and King. I understand they were working a couple of cases that might be dangerous," said Andy.

"I'm not sure how much help I can be," replied Witcher. "You know Pete's files are confidential."

"I understand that but I thought you might be able to tell me what he was working on that might cause someone to want to kill him."

"I really don't have any idea," responded Witcher. "It might be better if you backed off and let the police to do their job."

Andy felt his temperature rising and decided the best thing for him to do would be to leave Witcher's office before he said something that might hurt Pete's future. "I want to thank you for your time and I will give your suggestion some thought," he said as he left Witcher's office.

+++++

Sanders called Captain Davis as soon as he got to the office. He wanted to check out the detectives that had been assigned to Pete's case. Davis told Sanders they were both a little green but they were good detectives. Davis even said, "I told them if they would work with you, you would probably teach them a couple of things."

Sanders had just hung up with Captain Davis when Margaret, the temporary secretary, called him to let him know Detectives Searcy and Melton had arrived to see him. "Send them in," said Sanders.

Sanders walked to his door and opened it in time to see the two men walking down the hall. "You two come in," Sanders said as he pointed to the two chairs in front of his desk. They introduced themselves and shook hands. After everyone was seated, Sanders asked, "Have you seen Pete yet?"

"No, we have talked to the hospital and they told us to come by around 1:30. We should be able to see him then," said Searcy.

Even though Sanders didn't know the detectives, he wanted to start out on the right foot. He said, "You know we are going to be protective of Pete, so be patient with us. I hope you will share your information with us and we will try to do the same. For now, I want you to know, I talked with Pete this morning. He didn't provide details, but he did tell me that he and Janie both felt that something might be going on at Sneed, Weeks and King."

"Did Pete have any ideas?"

"No. The nurse ran me out before he could add anything else. His mother told me he had not talked about the shooting with anyone else."

+++++

The Dover Clan met in the hospital cafeteria for lunch and for an update. It seemed Pete was doing better than expected, but it was going to be a few days before he would be able to go home. Sue was insisting that he go to their house when he was released. Stan had talked with Pete and told him that he would be going to Jackson in the morning for Janie's funeral services. "I didn't have the heart to tell him his old boss, Weeks, didn't seem to know anything. I have to tell you Pete questioned me like he had me on the witness stand. I bet he is a good lawyer."

Andy agreed. "He wanted to know what I had learned about the shooting. He forced me to tell him we had not learned much. I didn't tell Pete, but I wasn't satisfied with my visit to his boss. She claimed everything was confidential. She wouldn't even give me the cases he was working on."

"I actually had a good visit with detectives Searcy and Melton," said Sanders. "They will be here at 1:30 to question Pete. I plan to be in the room when that happens."

Sue responded, "I'm glad you'll be here. But I have discovered, Pete can take care of himself."

The conversation went on for another thirty minutes before everyone left to take care of their assignments.

+++++

At 1:30 Sanders met Searcy and Melton outside Pete's room. The three of them entered his room together. Sanders introduced the detectives and said, "Pete, I'm here with Searcy and Melton because I wanted you to know that we are trying to work together. We want to find out who did this and we figure the best way to do that is to share as much information as we can."

"I understand that and I'll do my best to work with all of you. Of course, you're going to have to give me a few days before I can do much."

Searcy said, "Pete, right now we need you to point us in the right direction. We only know that someone driving a dark gray Mercury shot you and killed Janie Albert. We found the car on the Wal-Mart parking lot, but it was clean. A Wal-Mart employee described the driver as a very attractive, small but well built woman. Can you give us anything else?"

"I can confirm it was a woman who shot me. She called me by name and when I turned toward her, she shot me. Really, that's all I know about the shooting."

"Do you know anyone who might want you dead?" asked Melton.

"I've been giving that a lot of thought. It could have been someone from the past, but to save my life I can't figure out who that would be. I wonder what was happening with Janie at Sneed, Weeks and King. We were going to talk about something that had her very upset, but the shooting happened before we got around to it. I got the feeling it had something to do with her job."

Sanders said, "Your dad went to see your boss, a Ms. Debra Witcher. She wasn't any help. Something about the files being confidential."

"And she is right. The files are confidential. There are some things I can't tell you. However, I can tell you what is on the public record. According to the court records, I have two cases on the calendar that might be important to this shooting. First, there is the case where Charles Schuler is charged with first degree murder. According to the Memphis news media, Charles is a bad guy involved in all kinds of illegal activity."

Melton spoke up, "I know this guy and the news reports were really too kind to him. He would kill anyone who gets in his way."

"I've been getting a lot of pressure to go easy on him," said Pete. "Then second, I have a case coming up of a supposedly 'good guy'. Robert Shelby owns a chain of supermarkets. He is a member of the city council. He may even be related to the Shelby's of Shelby County. The FBI has put together a case charging him with 'money laundering'. The powers that be would like for this case to simply go away. However, the evidence I have is solid and should be followed up in court."

The detectives assured Pete this gave them somewhere to start their investigation and given time, they would find the person who killed Janie and tried to kill him.

Sanders stayed with Pete after the detectives left. As soon as they were out the door, Sanders said, "Tell me more about the firm you worked for before going to work for Justice."

+++++

Since Carol's boyfriend had already gone to work when she got back to Atlanta, she took a shower and went to bed. It had been an easy job. She had made the drive to Memphis, checked out the Wal-mart parking lot to make sure the 2004 dark gray Mercury Grand Marquis with a Texas tag number 886 TWC was parked there as promised. Everything had gone perfect until she got the phone call on the way back to Atlanta. How could he still be alive?

Carol ran to answer her private cell phone. The caller said, "Word is that Pete will get out of the hospital in a couple of days. There has been a guard in front of his door until now. However, now that he is out of ICU, I'm not sure how long that will last."

"What do you want me to do?" asked Carol.

"My desire has not changed. I asked you to take care of both of them and I still want him dead. If you can't do it, I will find someone who can."

"I can do it. When do you want it done?"

"I've been thinking about that. I believe it will be better to wait for some of the heat to die down. Give me a week or two and I'll get back to you with a plan."

"I'll be waiting for your call."

+++++

Stan and his wife, Pat, were on their way to Jackson, MS. The funeral service for Janie wasn't until 2:00 p.m. but they had an appointment with Janie's parents at 10:00 this morning. Stan had been assigned the task of trying to determine if Janie might have been the target. He had not been able to find out anything at Sneed, Weeks and King yesterday. In fact Weeks had been very cold and uncaring.

Pat was reading her husband's mind and asked, "What do you hope to learn from the Alberts?"

"Three things: First, Pete seems to believe there is some funny business going on at that law firm. I'd like to find out if Janie had said anything to her parents about anything at work. Second, I want to know if there was anything going on in Janie's personal life that could cause someone to want to kill her. Finally, I want to know what kind of relationship Janie and Pete had."

"Stan, remember they have just lost their daughter. They are filled with shock and grief. Please, be nice."

"I will. Just don't make me promise to be nice to Bob Wilkins."

"Who is Bob Wilkins?" asked Pat.

"Bob Wilkins was the person Janie was doing research for at Sneed, Weeks and King. It's hard for me to be objective about them. I felt like they were giving me the brush-off and I didn't like it."

Chapter Three

Helena-West Helena, AR
Mike's New Truck
June 14

    While Helena-West Helena is in Arkansas, it is more like an old plantation town in Mississippi. It is the county seat and the largest city in Phillips County, Arkansas. It had its beginning as a fort for the Confederate Army and there was a major battle fought there. It is located at the southern end of Crowley's Ridge, a geographic anomaly of the typically flat Arkansas Delta on the west and extends to the Mississippi River on the eastern side of Crowley's Ridge. The Helena Bridge, one of Arkansas' four Mississippi River bridges, carries U.S. Route 69 across to Mississippi.

    Today, Helena-West Helena is home to just over 12,000 people. The racial makeup of the city is one third White and two thirds African American. With a median income of $19,896 for a household, the city is one of the poorest in the nation. The chief economic influence continues to be agriculture, specifically cotton cultivation. Barge traffic at the city's port on the Mississippi River is another significant factor, in addition to retail and tourism.

    With this environment, it is easy to see how the area became a hot-bed for criminal activity. The Mississippi River

Bridge and barge traffic were perfect for drug trafficking. After 20 years of worsening crime and allegations of corruption in the Police Department, the new Mayor, Ron Washington and new Police Chief, Thomas Wells went to U.S. Attorney, Charles Peeler, to beg for federal help. Peeler assured Washington and Wells something would be done.

+++++

Ruby Shipman had been working for the Martin Ford dealership for about a month. Even though Ruby was now in her late thirties, she still had that slim shapely body with long blond hair that turned the heads of most of the men who saw her walk the dealership lot. Ruby had no doubt that her looks had everything to do with the fact she was already the leading salesperson for the company.

However, Ruby was actually Ruby Falls, an undercover FBI Agent who had spent most of her career in the New Orleans area. The FBI had set her up with a past. If anyone was trying to discover who she was, they would discover that Ruby Shipman was from St. Louis, MO. She had moved to Helena with her boyfriend. However, they had broken up leaving her to find her own way in Helena. In her past in St Louis she had several minor problems with the law. Ruby Falls' new assignment was to investigate the drug trafficking on both sides of the Mississippi River around Helena. Her job was to infiltrate the criminal element and find out the leaders of drug trafficking and criminal activity in the area. Ruby was to report her findings to Pete Dover.

Ruby had just completed the sale of a new four door 150 Ford to Mike Weston. Mike was a 38 year old single stud who was still in good shape from his days playing football at Ole Miss. Mike was 6 foot 3 and had brown hair. He was dressed in blue jeans with a flannel gray shirt and black engineer boots. In the process of selling the pick up, Ruby had let it be known that she might be available for some after hour activity. Mike's father, Leon Wesson, was one of the big farmers in the area and Ruby figured Mike must work with his dad. There was also a lot of talk that Mike's real money came from working with some suspicious characters.

Just before Mike left Martin Ford, he finally said, "Since I bought the truck from you, you know you owe me."

Playing dumb Ruby asked, "What do you mean?"

"Well, we're having a big party Saturday night out at the Island. Would you be interested in going?"

It turned out the party was to be on "Big Island" which is an island in the middle of the Mississippi River about 25 miles below the Helena slack water harbor. Years ago the island had been a very upscale deer hunting club. Today it is an exclusive club. Membership is limited and very expensive. Both Mississippi and Arkansas claimed "Big Island." But the truth is neither state has paid much attention to the goings on of the Island. There are all kinds of rumors as to what takes place on "Big Island" today. Ruby had heard about the parties that took place there and thought this just might be a way to get on the inside with the people involved in drug trafficking and criminal activity in the area.

"I would love to go. I haven't done much since I have been here and it would be good to get out of the rut of going home every night, watching a little television and then going to bed alone. I have gone to the casino across the bridge into Mississippi a few times."

Mike responded, "I'll pick you up around 8:00 this evening. What is your address?"

After giving Mike her address of 135 Court Street, he left the lot and Ruby began to wonder if she had made a mistake. Her major issue was the fact that she would be without transportation except for her date. It had always been important to her to have an exit plan. In this situation, if things got to rough for her, she didn't have a way out and the more she thought about, the more it bothered her. "Oh well," she thought, "it was three days until Saturday; maybe she could figure something out."

+++++

Mike knew it would be alright to bring a guest to the party, however, he decided to make a trip to Big Island and have a drink and let the leaders of the club know he was bringing a guest and who she was. Since Ruby had not lived in Helena-West Helena long, Mike felt no one would know her and he didn't want to get in trouble with Frank Castle who controlled everything that happened on Big Island.

Actually, Frank Castle, Joe Cole, and Mike's dad, Leon, were the "powers" in charge of the Club. Frank Castle was the front man who lived on Big Island and was the "go to" person. However, Joe Cole and Leon Wesson were just as powerful. Joe was a leading attorney who lived in Helena and kept the Club out of trouble with the local law. He also had some kind of connections in Memphis. Leon was a wealthy farmer and was on the board of directors of First Bank of Helena as well as the Planter Bank of West Helena. These three men controlled not only the Club but just about all of Phillips County.

As Mike crossed the bridge that took him to Big Island, he remembered back to a time before the bridge. To get to Big Island then, you had to take a boat. As a boy, he thought that had been fun. He was forever sorry they had managed get the county judge to put in the bridge. It took something of the mystery of the Island away.

Since it was noon when Mike entered the restaurant he planned to have a steak to go along with his drink. He immediately saw his dad along with Frank Castle. "Come over and eat lunch with us," Frank yelled.

"Be right there," said Mike, "after I speak to Susie." Susie was the waitress that Mike had been out with a few times. With a wink at Susie, Mike said, "bring me a steak, baked potato, salad, and a good cold Bud."

As Mike sat down with Frank and his dad he realized he was interrupting a conversation about the "pawn shop". It seems the "pawn shop" is a part of the Club that receives stolen items from the locals and transports them to other states for sale. Mike's dad was in charge of this work for the Club and he had just completed talking with the drivers who were transporting the stolen items north to a dealer who would sell them. They were taking two loaded 18 wheelers which would bring the club $1,250,000 income.

"When are the trucks leaving?" asked Mike.

"One will be pulling out around 4:00 a.m. on Monday and one will leave thirty minutes later. Mike, I want you to take that new pick-up of yours and lead the way, 500 miles north to Chicago. You have two jobs. First, make sure the first truck picks up the stuff at the warehouse in Memphis. We left room for about half a truck load. Second, stay in contact with both drivers and make sure there are no traps that have been set up for them. When you get there, collect the money but before you pay the drivers, call us and we'll have a load for them to pick up and bring back to Memphis. There is no need for you to lead them back."

"No problem, I'll be here and ready around 3:30 Monday morning. Speaking of my new truck, the girl who sold it to me is quite a 'looker'. Her name is Ruby Shipman and I plan to bring her to the party Saturday night."

"What do you know about her?" asked Frank.

"I know she sold me a truck and she looks like someone I would like to get to know better."

"I'll check her out this afternoon, just to be sure," said Frank.

Mike wondered if the stuff coming up the river had been delivered, but he didn't ask. He knew Frank and his dad would tell him what he needed to know when he needed to know it.

Chapter Four

Memphis, TN
Operation Delta Pride
June 13

    Pete had been released from the hospital and had agreed to stay at his mom and dad's for a few days. However, he was about to climb the wall. He wanted to get involved with the investigation as well as the cases on his desk. Finally, he gave in to the urge and called Sanders. "Sanders, can you come by mom's as soon as possible. I need you to catch me up on what is going on."

    "Sure, I can be there by 3:00 this afternoon," answered Sanders as he hung up the phone. Sanders knew Pete well enough to know what was on his mind. He wanted to get out in the field and help catch the shooter. And Sanders didn't blame him. He knew what was on Pete's mind because that is exactly what he would have been feeling about this time. Sanders only had a couple of calls to make and then he would head over to see Pete.

    His first call was to Detective Jerry Searcy. He wanted to see if Searcy had any new information so he could report to Pete. Searcy had nothing. In fact he had told Sanders that everywhere they turned they ran into a dead-end. Sanders just hoped that Detective Jerry Searcy was sharing his information with him as agreed.

It was 2:40 p.m. when Pete asked Sanders to come in. Sanders commented on how good Pete looked and followed him. Pete led him to a bedroom that had been empty the last time Sanders had been in the house. However, today it was filled with all the office equipment that Pete might need to do his work. Pete sat behind the desk and asked Sanders to set in the comfortable platform rocker.

As expected, Pete began by asking Sanders to update him on the investigation. However, not as expected, it was easy for Sanders to see that Pete had already gone back to work. It's true that he was still in his mom's house, but the computer and files had been brought in from his office in the justice building. Pete was working.

Sanders began by telling Pete that not much was happening with the case. He had just talked with Detective Searcy who had told him that everywhere they looked they ran into a dead-end. "When your grandpa went to Janie's funeral he met with her mom and dad. They had the feeling that Janie had stumbled on to something at work that may have gotten her killed."

"I think they are right. She called me to ask my advice on what to do with some information she had discovered. We had been friends for a long time and had gone out a few times, however, there was no sparks. We were simply good friends. In any case, we decided to take in a play and then come back to my place and talk it through. I wish I knew what had been on her mind, but I don't."

"Do you know anything else that I should know?" asked Sanders.

"Yes, and I need to tell you but I can't."

"What do you mean, you can't? How can we get to the bottom of this if you're keeping things from us?"

"Sanders, Justice is working on a big case involved in all sorts of criminal activities. The code name for the case is 'Operation Delta Pride'. We have an uncover agent in the mix and the agent reports to me. I'm afraid if I tell you more I will endanger the agent's life."

"Damn fire --- that puts a new light on the whole thing. You think someone has discovered who the agent is and that he is connected to you?"

"I don't know what to think. I heard from the agent just before I was shot. Sanders, you used to work with the FBI, what should I do?"

"I'd bet my left arm this whole thing is somehow connected with the shooting. I don't know how, but I bet it is. Pete, you have to tell me who the agent is and what his mission is."

"You know I could loose my job."

"You could loose your life and the agent's life. Janie is already dead. Let me get involved."

Pete thought he may have already said too much. At the same time he knew Sanders well enough to know he would not let it go. Sanders would keep after him until he told him the whole story. It seemed he really didn't have much of a choice.

"Okay, but I need to warn you, I don't know how it all fits together yet. Shortly after I went to work for Justice I was assigned to a new Task Force made up of Western District of Tennessee, Northern District of Mississippi and the Eastern District of Arkansas. The task force is called the Narcotics and Organized Crime Drug Enforcement Task Force. (OCDETF). I am one of the attorneys who prosecute the cases. However, I was also given some field responsibilities. I have already prosecuted two cases. One involved a Boliver man who was sentenced for drug trafficking. The other one involved a Barlett doctor who pled guilty to unlawfully distributing prescription drugs."

"My god, Pete, you have been making all kinds of enemies."

"I don't believe either of these cases were the cause for the shooting. I believe the shooting somehow involves Operation Delta Pride and the drug trafficking and criminal activity in our three districts. It's big! The uncover agent in Helena reports to me and it is our job to identify the leaders of this drug trafficking and develop evidence which will allow Justice to get a conviction and take a big bite out of drug trafficking in the area."

"Does this investigation involve Janie in any way? Why was she killed? Has someone made the connection between you and the investigation? Is this why you were shot?"

"Those are my questions. I really don't know," responded Pete.

Chapter Five

Memphis Airport
Contraband
June 14

"Did you get the stuff out of the last Southwest plane," Victor asked. Victor was a baggage handler who worked part-time making sure five other handlers collected items stolen from the baggage and drugs which had been hidden behind special panels of the incoming planes at the Memphis airport.

Jack answered, "Yeah, I got it and put it in the bank. By the way the bank is about full, we need to make a delivery."

The bank was the "safe place" in the Memphis Airport where the baggage handlers put the contraband that was being stolen from baggage or taken from hidden compartments located in the incoming planes. Items taken by baggage handlers included: laptops, fine clothing, perfume, liquor and all kinds of electronics, as well as, the cocaine from the hidden compartments. In the last year, deliveries from the bank had brought six baggage handlers $1,400,000.

Jack felt that there was as much as $300,000 worth of stuff in the bank now. It was Victor's job to move the stuff and get the money. He had the contacts and had done a good job. Jack and the others had sure enjoyed the money. Victor took his 50% off the top and the other five baggage handlers split the rest. That meant in the last year Jack had received $140,000 from his "part time" job. That was not bad. However, he had begun to wonder if Victor's 50% wasn't too much.

Victor had already made the arrangements for the stuff to be picked up at 1:00 a.m. Sunday morning. It would be picked up by a L & L Laundry truck. L & L picked up and delivered laundry to the airport all the time and their truck at the airport wasn't unusual. Victor had no idea where the driver took the stuff. He did know that he got paid well for what he did. He managed the five baggage handler and made a phone call and for that he was paid $700,000 last year. He wasn't complaining.

Victor's contact person had made the arrangement for the stuff at the airport to be picked up and taken to a warehouse large enough for the truck to simple drive in. After delivering the loaded truck, the driver was to be paid and leave the truck.

+++++

On Thursday night, Albert "Al" Eason was working at his job as an air-traffic controller at the Memphis airport. Al was the son of Gracie Sanders and the grandson of Stan Dover of the Dover Detective Agency. He had been working at the airport for four years and loved his job. Maybe that was because he met some of the most attractive women while he was working. As he worked, he was thinking about one woman named Sally. She had beautiful long brown hair; legs that he dreamed about being locked around him; small and firm breast that were enough to satisfy any man. Just thinking about looking into her blue eyes made Al want to take off from work and try to find her.

Sally was a pilot for the Southwest Airline plane that had just landed. Al had a break coming up in fifteen minutes. Therefore, he decided to give her a call and see if she would meet him for lunch. Al had an hour and a half for his break.

Thinking about Sally made him want to see her—real bad. He dialed her number and listened as it rang four times.

"Can I call you right back?" Sally said as she answered his call.

"I'll be waiting."

In less than five minutes Al's phone rang, "Sorry I couldn't talk. What's on your mind?"

"I know you just got off the plane from Dallas and I have a lunch break at 1:00 a.m. I wondered if we could have lunch together."

"Where do you want to meet?"

"What about Shorty Small's, I believe they are open all night?" In Al's opinion Shorty Small's had the best food in the airport.

+++++

Sally was late. Al had been outside Shorty Small's for twenty minutes and he was impatient. After all he didn't have all night. He had to go back to work at 2:30. Finally, when he could stand it no longer he dialed Sally's number.

"Sorry I'm late but something is going on. Could you come around to the Southwest gate?"

"Sure, I'll be right there," answered Al as he hung up his phone.

Sally was standing in front of the large windows which overlooked the runway when Al arrived at the Southwest gate. She waved for him to come over.

"What's going on?" Al asked.

"I'm not sure. I noticed that after the baggage handlers finished delivering the bags to the baggage area, they came back to the plane and have been unloading other things from the planes. They loaded the baggage train and took it to the other side of the airport and now they are back for another load. What could they be doing?"

"I don't know but I would bet everything I have that they are up to no good. Let me call Sanders and see if he has time to come and check it out."

By the time Sanders arrived at the airport the baggage handlers were gone. Al apologized to Sanders for getting him out in the middle of the night and then told him their story and asked what he thought.

"I don't know for sure but I would guess the plane was carrying some kind of private merchandise that the airline knew nothing about. Do you have any idea where they took the merchandise?"

"Neither Sally nor I could figure it out. It seemed they just disappeared and when they came back the baggage train was empty."

"Let me walk around and see if I can discover anything."

"Sounds good to me," said Sally, "we don't want to report it to the airline until we are convinced that something illegal is going on."

"Sanders, I have to go back to work in forty-five minutes. In the meantime, I need to get something to eat. Can you let us know what you find?"

"Sure, I'll get back to you later today."

In silence, Sally and Al walked around to Shorty Small's and ordered. It was 1:45 a.m. and there was no one in the restaurant except Sally and Al and they were very quiet as they waited for their food.

+++++

Victor watched as Sanders walked across the tarmac in the direction that Al had told him the baggage train had gone.

Victor had no idea who the strange man on the tarmac was but he knew he shouldn't be there. He called security and told them there was an unauthorized man walking away from Southwest Airline's gate.

As Sanders approached the western edge of the airport tarmac, the security guard was walking toward him. Sanders could see that he was approaching him and that this would not be a fun meeting.

"Hey, fellow, what are you doing out here?" ask the security guard when he got close enough.

"I'm just walking around, trying to get some air. I have a four hour layover before my plane leaves," answered Sanders.

"Well, you can't walk out here. You could get run over by an incoming plane."

Sanders gave a wave to the guard and then began to walk back into the airport. He was sure something was going on and wondered what he could do. He decided to get back with Al and suggest that the three of them take turns watching incoming Southwest planes. With the investigation into Pete's shooting, Sanders knew he didn't have a lot of free time, so Sally and Al would need to do most of the work.

Chapter Six

Memphis
Dover Detective Agency
June 15

Friday morning the Dover Detective Agency was having its regular "catch up" meeting. This was the time when all members of the agency shared what was happening with their part of any investigation in which the agency was involved. Andy, the oldest son, was CEO of the firm and was leading the meeting. "Sam, let's start with you. How is the Casidy case coming along?"

"As you know Dennis Casidy, has asked us to investigate a possible embezzling case. I have discovered that David Jump, one of the partners in the car dealership has been cooking the books. My findings have been shared with Dennis. Now, all I have to do is gather enough evidence to prove that David is the guilty party. I should have the case wrapped up in about a week."

It was obvious that the other members of the firm were preoccupied with the shooting that involved Janie Albert and Pete Dover. Therefore, the meeting moved on with Andy asking, "Does anyone have anything new on the shooting?"

Sue said, "As Pete's mom, I can tell you he is out of the hospital and staying at my house for a while. He is recovering very nicely. He is still weak and has to rest some during the day but he has forced us to make him an office out of the empty bedroom. He is already working too hard."

Sanders was listening to Sue but his mind was on his conversation with Pete. How much should he share with the group? He was caught between loyalties. He owed it to Andy and Sue to let them know what he knew. However, he had promised Pete he would keep their conversation private. Finally he spoke up, "I met with Pete yesterday afternoon. We spent most of our time trying to tie the shooting to his work at Justice or Janie's work at the law firm. I don't know that I am any closer to an answer than I was before." There, he had told the truth. He just had not told the "whole" truth.

"Before I forget it, I got a call from Al at the airport. It seems that there is something, possibly something illegal, going on there. I am working with him and Sally to see if we can discover what's happening."

"Who's Sally?" asked Gracie.

"I don't know for sure but I had the feeling there was something going on between her and Al. I do know she is a pilot for Southwest Airlines."

There were questions about Pete, as well as the airport, but most of the conversation was more personal than business and the meeting was soon adjourned.

Chapter Seven

Big Island
The Date
June 16

It was Saturday night and Ruby was expecting Mike to pick her up any minute. Since being inviting to the party at Big Island, Ruby had been talking to people at the dealership. No one had been to Big Island but they had heard a lot about it --- most of it bad. It seemed that there had been people who went there, never to be heard from again.

Ruby's emotions were all over the place. She always felt an excitement when about to do something that could be dangerous and Ruby was convinced there were things about Big Island that could be dangerous to her. And Mike presented a different kind of danger altogether. She had to admit she was attracted to him. How was she going to handle it when he wanted her to go to bed with him? As an undercover agent, she had long ago made the decision that she would go to bed with a man, if necessary, in order to do her job. Ruby was also experiencing the emotion of fear. It was a fear of the unknown. It was a fear of not being in control.

In the middle of allowing her mind to wander, Ruby's phone rang. Her caller ID told her it was Pete. She really didn't have time to talk to him. A part of her didn't want to answer the phone. Although she had never met Pete, they had talked several times on the phone. "Hey, Pete," Ruby said as she finally answered the phone.

"Ruby, you got a minute."

"Just barely, my date is to pick me up in fifteen minutes."

"Then let me make this quick. You may not know but I was shot last week and just got out of the hospital. I am laid up at my mom and dad's. I don't think so but it could have had something to do with Operation Delta Pride."

"Are you alright? What do you think I should do?"

"I'm going to be alright. Just homebound for now. You should be very careful and we need to meet as soon as possible. Give me a call when you can come to Memphis without it being noticed."

Interrupting Pete, Ruby said, "Gotta go, the door bell is ringing."

"I'm almost ready, let me get my wrap," Ruby said as she opened the door for Mike. Mike was dressed in dark gray dress pants and a light blue short sleeved shirt. He looked very handsome in a casual sort of way.

"I haven't seen you wear that outfit at the dealership," responded Mike as he took a good look at his date. She had on the "little black dress" that every woman should have, low cut with plenty of cleavage showing, thin straps holding it up, and three inch heels. "Are you sure you want to go to the party. We could just stay here and make out."

As Ruby was slipping her arm into her coat she said, "No way, I haven't been to a party in months. I'm ready to go."

"And I haven't had sex in months. We could do both."

"Not now, I don't believe you and besides I want to dance," Ruby said as she opened the door. Reluctantly, Mike followed her. After locking the door, she turned to see that he was driving the new truck that she had sold him earlier in the week.

+++++

Ruby didn't know what she expected but Big Island was more elegant than anything she had imagined. As soon as they crossed the bridge they begin to see homes that had been built on the island. Mike told Ruby these were "second" homes for many club members. Very few people lived on Big Island full time. All the buildings were made from logs with a lot of glass. They were a long way from what she thought of as a log cabin. At the end of the road was a massive club house where the party was being held. On the outside it was logs with a lot of glass and some stone trim.

It was almost 9:00 p.m. and the party was in full swing. The live band was playing 50's music. Mike escorted Ruby to a table close to the dance floor and then went to get drinks for the both of them. Ruby was spending her time listening to the music and people watching while Mike was gone. He had been gone longer than she expected when she saw him talking to an older man. She really wished she could hear what they were saying.

"The background check on Ruby Shipman came back okay," said Frank Castle.

"I'm glad," responded Clyde, "I think she is someone I would really like to know better."

"Just be careful how much you tell her or let her see."

"Oh, I will. Tonight she came to dance so I'd better get back with her drink."

+++++

It was 2:15 a.m. when Mike pulled the truck up in front of Ruby's apartment. Ruby knew Mike would expect to come in and take her to bed. She had learned early in her career with the FBI that it was sometimes necessary to go to bed with a suspect in order to get the necessary information and besides that, she was attracted to this man and would probably enjoy the sex. However, tonight was not the night. In order to avoid a scene she faked being sick from drinking too much. Mike wasn't too happy; however, after she had upchucked as she was getting out of the truck, he accepted it.

The truth was Ruby had drunk more than she should have but she was having fun. The band was very good and she had really enjoyed herself. By keeping her eyes and ears open she had learned a few things that could be helpful later. Mike had introduced her to Frank Castle and Joe Cole. Mike told her Frank lived on the island and was in charge of the Club while Joe was the attorney for the Club. Ruby found Frank to be loud and controlling. Joe was very quiet. She had always heard it was the quiet ones you had to watch out for. All in all, Ruby felt it had been a productive night.

Chapter Eight

Memphis Airport
Observing
June 16

     Al watched as the 1:00 a.m. Southwest Airline plane set down on the Memphis International Airport runway. Al was using his day off to try to figure out what was happening with the baggage handlers. Since Sally was piloting this plane, he would get a chance to see her. He had gone by Wendy's and picked up a burger and fries for the both of them. Because they were spending so much time watching the baggage handlers, Al had missed being with Sally. Their work schedule seemed to make it impossible for them to have any quality time together.

     Al watched as the baggage was unloaded, loaded on the train and brought to the baggage area. Nothing exciting seemed to be going on with them. However, the excitement began to pick up when Al saw Sally walking up the off ramp. She had to know he was watching her. No one could walk that sexy naturally. She waved and said she would be right there.

     By the time Sally arrived, Al had found a table and spread out their food and drink. The table was in front of the big window so they could keep an eye on the tarmac and the baggage handlers.

After a big hug and a short kiss, Al asked about Sally's flight from Dallas.

"It was pretty routine. Nothing exciting and that is just the way I like it," said Sally. "How about the baggage handlers? What's happening here?"

"I just noticed that after taking the baggage to the baggage area they have gone back to the plane for something." Just then, the baggage train made its appearance but instead of bringing baggage to the baggage area, it went in the opposite direction. The train only had a few items on it. It was headed in the same direction that it had gone the other night when Al and Sally had watched it. Leaving their food on the table, this time they intended to follow the train and try to discover what was going on.

It didn't take long. The train pulled into an old hanger building. The building looked as though it had been deserted for years. The front of the building was open with an old, small plane stored in it. In the back on the right side of the building, Al and Sally could see an enclosed area. It looked like an old "portable building" had been moved into the back of the hanger building.

As Sally and Al got closer, they could see an L & L Laundry truck backed up to the enclosed area. Two men were loading something into the truck. Victor had parked the baggage train so Jack could unload it into the truck. In an effort to get a better view of the action, Sally and Al moved to the opening of the hanger building. They still couldn't see what was being loaded. They needed to get closer. As they started to move closer still, Sally tripped on a ladder and made it fall which made an awful noise.

"Did you hear that?" asked Victor.

"I heard something," answered Jack.

The two men in the truck continued to load. It was apparent they had not heard anything. Victor and Jack looked around to see what had made the racket while Sally and Al were able to slip out of the hanger.

"That was close," said Sally.

"I thought Victor had seen us," responded Al. "I wonder where the truck is taking all that stuff?" Since the men had been loading the truck, Al sent Sally after her car so they could follow the truck.

About fifteen minutes later, Al heard the baggage train start up. Then he saw Victor driving the train out of the hanger. "Where was Sally?" he said aloud. Then he saw her. He ran toward the car as the laundry truck was pulling out of the hanger building.

"Follow that truck," Al said as he slid in the car with Sally.

Chapter Nine

Big Island
The Trip North
June 16

Mike arrived at the Pawn Shop at 4:00 a.m., just as they had completed loading the eighteen wheelers.

"I was about to leave without you," shouted Vic, the lead driver.

Mike laughed and shouted back, "I wanted to be sure the work was all done. Let me check with dad and then I'll be ready to get this show on the road."

As Mike walked into the office of the Pawn Shop, Leon said, "Damn son, can't you get anywhere on time?" You should be half way to Memphis by now."

Mike could see his dad was pissed. He simply asked, "Anything I need to know before I leave?"

"Lead Vic to the warehouse in Memphis. Get the doors open so he can pull the truck inside. There are two men waiting to load. The two of you could help. Pay the men and get back on the road as soon as you can. I want you and Vic to be ahead of Woodie, so I plan to hold his truck here until 5:00 a.m. That should give you time to get Vic loaded and back on the road."

"What do you think I should be able to get for both loads including the cocaine from Memphis?"

"At least half a million, maybe more, for the pawn shop items and twice that much for the cocaine. Call me when you have the money. By the way, when you get back we need to talk about moving the stuff we have here."

"Okay, I'm out of here," Mike said as he left the office and headed for his truck.

+++++

Sally followed the laundry truck to a warehouse just off South I-55 at 4689 Brooks Road. Al asked her to pull up to the curb so they could watch and wait. The doors of the warehouse opened, the truck drove in and the doors closed. Sally and Al waited for the men to come out of the warehouse. However, instead of the men coming out, a new red F150 Ford pickup with Arkansas plates and an eighteen wheeler pulled up and the doors opened again.

Al said, "I'm going to call Sanders. We need someone to tell us what to do now."

"I agree."

Sanders answered on the fifth ring, "Sanders."

"Sanders this is Al. Sally is here with me and we have been watching the baggage train at the airport and we need some advice."

"What's happening?"

Al told Sanders what had been going on since about 1:00 a.m. and after listening intently Sanders said, "I think the three of us need to get together with Pete this morning. It could be that he would know something about this. Let me call him and set up a meeting at Andy's for 10:00 a.m. I'll call you back if that won't work with Pete.

Al and Sally planned to watch and wait for another thirty minutes at least. No telling what would happen next. However, they didn't have to wait that long. At 6:10 the doors of the warehouse opened again. The pickup was the first out and right behind it was the eighteen wheeler. Sally had paper and pencil ready and wrote down the license numbers of both vehicles. Then the laundry truck pulled through the doors and stopped. The passenger got out and closed and locked the overhead doors before getting back in the truck. Sally also got that license number.

+++++

It was 6:30 a.m. and Mike and the two eighteen wheelers were out of Memphis and looking forward to a nine hour drive. Mike felt the stop in Memphis had been uneventful. The four men were able to transfer the merchandise in no time, the men were paid, and the trucks were on their way to Chicago. Mike felt that trip should also be uneventful. Neither truck had any maintenance issues---neither was over the weight limit---both drivers had been instructed to drive under the speed limit. Yes, Mike expected a calm trip as he turned up the country music on the radio. His job was to look out for troopers and make sure the drivers knew where they were.

As he listened to the country singers sing about their love life, he couldn't help remember his Saturday night date with Ruby. He wasn't happy about not getting any but he had to admit she had been a lot of fun. She was a good dancer and was attractive enough that all the men in The Club kept looking her over. Talking to himself he asked, "Why didn't I ask her to take this trip with me? After the delivery, we could have shacked up in a motel and I could have got in her pants."

Just then he saw it---there was a trooper behind that grove of trees. Immediately he looked to see how fast he was going. Oh shit, nine miles over. He had been daydreaming and not watching his speed. Watching the trooper as he passed even with it, he noticed the blue lights had not come on yet. Maybe he would get lucky. He held his breath, still no lights. He had slowed down to seventy and made himself a promise to keep the speed control set at seventy. Then he took out his cell phone and called Vic who should be about fifteen minutes behind him.

Vic answer with, "what's up?"

"I just passed a trooper on the right in a grove of trees. Be careful and call Woodie and let him know."

"Will do and thanks."

+++++

At 10:00 a.m. Al and Sally were knocking on Pete's front door. They had noticed Sanders' car was already parked in the driveway. As Pete opened the front door he invited them back to his temporary office. Sanders was seated in a large wing-back chair. Pete had brought in two dinning room chairs for Al and Sally while he sat behind the desk.

After the introductions were made between Sally and Pete, Pete said, "Sanders has brought me up to date as to the problems at the airport. Did anything happen after 6:00 a.m.?"

"Oh yes! Let me get my notes," said Sally. After getting the notes Sally began to read, "At 6:10 the doors of the warehouse opened again. The pickup was the first out and right behind it was the eighteen wheeler. The pickup looked new and had been sold by Martin Ford in Helena AR. Its license number is Arkansas 351 APU. The eighteen wheeler had an Arkansas tag number 782 CEW. We were about to leave when the L & L laundry truck came out. It had a Tennessee tag number ERC 895. They must have been the last out because they locked up after closing the overhead doors."

Are you sure it was an L & L laundry truck?"

"No doubt about it. However, neither the driver nor the passenger was wearing uniforms," replied Al.

Sanders couldn't help it, he said, "Pete, I don't know how this all fits with your being shot. But the hair on the back of my neck tells me it is connected."

"I don't know. At this point I don't see how." Pete didn't want to mention the fact that there was an FBI agent in West Helena who was working uncover. Only Sanders knew about her and Pete wasn't ready to expand that number just yet.

"What should we do now?" asked Al.

"The two of you keep watching and keep me informed. Right now, let me call in these license numbers. I'll ask the state troopers to pull them over for a routine check. Maybe something will turn up.

As the group was breaking up and about to leave, Pete was able to tell Sanders to wait. He had something he needed to talk over with him.

Going back into his temporary office, Pete said, "I didn't want to bring it up in front of the others but I know you noticed the pickup was sold in Helena and surely you remembered we have an undercover agent there. I am wondering what you make of this coincidence."

"First, I don't believe in coincidences. Second, there must be a connection. I think you need to talk to the agent. At least let him know what is going on here."

"The agent is not a 'him'. She called me last week and we decided we needed to meet as soon as she could get away. Today, she called just before you got here and she is on her way. She is to be here by 1:00 p.m. Do you have any advice for me?"

"Not really, but the two of you need to be careful. I really believe Al and Sally are on to something and since that pickup was from Helena it has to be connected somehow. I will continue to work with them." As Sanders got up to leave he said, "Let me know if I can do anything."

Sanders had almost got to the front door when Pete called. "Sanders, come back a minute. I need some personal advice."

Returning to Pete's office, Sanders said, "I can tell you what to do but don't hold me responsible for your actions."

"Living here with Mom and Dad is about to drive me up the wall. I know Mom means well, so I don't want to hurt her feelings. I have another month or so before I can go back to the office. I wondered what you thought about me moving back into my apartment and bringing one of the temp's from the Department of Justice to help me."

"That could work and it just may be that Sue and Andy will be as glad to have their privacy back as much as you will. Is there someone at the office that you trust enough to deal with your sensitive issues?"

"I've been thinking about it and there is a second year intern who has been doing some work for me. She would be able to pick things up quickly and go with them. If you think this might work, I could talk to Mom and Dad tonight and my boss tomorrow. By the way, can you check up on the L & L Laundry truck? If there is a connection with the shooting, I may need you to be my legs for a while."

"No problem. I'll get right on it and I'll stay close to Al and Sally."

+++++

Pete's phone rang and it was Ruby. "I will be at your place in about fifteen minutes."

"Sounds good to me. I'll be here. In fact, I'll leave the front door open. Just open it, step in, and yell. " Since the shooting I move very slowly."

Pete was clearing some of the junk mail off his desk when he heard the front door open and a woman yell, "Pete".

Pete yelled back, "I'm in the room to the left after you take the first right into the hall. Come on back." He heard her walking toward his office.

Even though Ruby was now in her late thirties, she still had that slim shapely body with long blond hair that turned the heads of most of the men who saw her. "I'm Ruby," she said as she came through the door.

Pete was on his feet and reaching out to shake hands with Ruby. "I'm Pete. Pour yourself a cup of coffee. As slow as I am it will be cold if I do it." Pete and Ruby spend some time getting to know each other before they got down to the business portion of their meeting.

Ruby told Pete about the Big Island party she attended and that she had met three power players: Frank Castle, who seemed to be the front man at Big Island; Joe Cole, a big time lawyer; and Leon Wesson, the biggest farmer in the area. "These three men seem to have control of just about everything in Phillips County."

Pete asked questions about the men and about Big Island. Then he began to update her about what he had learned from Sally and Al. When he mentioned a new red 150 Ford pickup which was sold in Helena, Ruby spoke up, "I think I sold that truck to Mike Wesson about ten days ago. Mike is the son of the big farmer, Leon Wesson. I went to the party on Big Island with him."

"Now we're getting somewhere. If Mike was leading an eighteen wheeler to Memphis and beyond there must be some connection to whatever is going on at the airport." Pete still had a lot of questions that need an answer but he felt at least some of the pieces were coming together. However, he had no idea if any of this had anything to do with the shooting. Before she left, Ruby agreed to establish a relationship with Mike and follow up with the power players.

+++++

Vic was just ten miles beyond Champaign, IL. He had been making good time and was within two hours of Chicago. Then he saw the blue lights. "Damn," he said aloud. He began to look for a place to pull over as he called Mike.

Mike said, "Stay calm and do everything by the book. You have an invoice that says you picked up your load in Memphis and it is to be delivered to McKnight Inc., 8117 Meadowbrook Lane, Chicago. The invoice says your load includes misc merchandise. Your log book is up to date. Tell the trooper you haven't seen the load and if he asks you to open the doors, you have to do it. Good luck and call me when you can."

Chapter Ten

Memphis
The Move
June 18

Pete's conversation with his parents about moving back to his apartment was not too confrontational. While his Mom was not happy about it, she understood and in fact, his parents had helped him make the move. Even his boss, Debra Witcher, felt it was the smart thing to do. As he closed the door behind his mom and dad, he found himself alone for the first time in what seemed like forever.

Debra had talked to Alice Hunter, a second year intern, about working for Pete at his apartment and his mom had hired a woman to keep the apartment clean and make sure he did not starve. Alice would be at the apartment at 2:00 p.m. to interview with Pete. As he began to prepare for the interview, Pete couldn't help but remember how attractive Alice was. She had blond hair with a very good figure. He would guess she was about 5'4" tall and might have weighted 130 pounds. In working with her before, Pete knew she was very smart and was able to pick things up quickly. Yes, he was looking forward to this new relationship.

Pete had made his way to the front door just as the door bell rang. He had known it would take a while for him to get from the office to the front door, so he had started early. What he saw when he opened the door was even more beautiful than his earlier day dreams. This was going to be interesting, Pete thought as he invited Alice back to his office. "It will take me a while to get to the office, so you might want to go ahead. It is the first door to the left." Pete was telling the truth, he moved so slow it would take a while for him to reach the office, but he also wanted to be behind Alice so he could watch her walk. He was not disappointed.

Once inside the office, Pete became very businesslike. "What did Debra tell you concerning the job here?"

"She told me that you would be working while you were recuperating at home and you would need someone to help with the details of your work. Debra said the work would be the same kind of office work I had been doing for you before you were shot and that you would need me about 20 hours a week."

"She's right. The work will be much like what you were doing. However, there will be some differences. As you can see I am still moving very slowly. There will times that I will need you to be my legs here in the apartment as well as run errands. I am working with an uncover agent and you will need to keep anything you learn confidential. You will keep a relationship with my secretary at the Department of Justice. I'm not sure how many hours I will need you but it should be somewhere between twenty and forty. Do you think this is something you would like to do for a month or so?"

"I think it could be an interesting change for me. When do you want me to start?"

"Is tomorrow too soon?"

"No. I can do that. I only have one loose end I will need to take care of soon. I was not aware of it until yesterday, but my apartment building is being shut down. I have to find a place to live."

Pete felt good about the interview and decided it was time to draw it to a close. Therefore, he stood and said, "Then I will see you at 8:00 in the morning. By the way, here is a key to the front door. Just ring the bell and come on in. I'm so slow; I'll let you let yourself out."

"Thanks, I will see you in the morning, replied Alice."

After Alice left, Pete wondered if he should have offered to let Alice stay in his apartment while they were working together. She had said most of her stuff was still at her mom's so she would be traveling light. He would have to think about it for a while. It would sure be handy for both of them, but would it bring on more problems than it was worth? He just didn't know.

+++++

It was 4:00 p.m. and time for a weekly "catch up" meeting of the Dover Detective Agency. Everyone was present when Andy opened the meeting with the announcement that Pete's health was progressing well and against his mother's wishes he was now back in his own apartment.

Then it was time for an update on the shooting which killed Janie and injured Pete. Andy reported that he had been investigating the cases of Charles Schuler and Robert Shelby. Charles Schuler is the bad guy being tried for murder and Robert Shelby is the grocery man who is charged with money laundering. Andy said, "At this point I have not been able to make a connection with either of them and the shooting. The Justice Department has assigned other attorneys to take their cases. Pete says that is normal but he is worried because he believes the department would like for the case against Shelby to simply go away."

Stan was next to report and his report had to do with Janie. "I have talked with Janie's parents again and they have no idea why she might have been killed. They do remember she had said something about something strange going on at work but they assumed she was simply killed because she was with an attorney for the Justice Department. I have also been to Sneed, Weeks and King to keep my appointment with Bob Wilkins who was Janie's immediate boss. I have to admit that I don't like the guy and I believe anything is possible with him. However, I didn't learn anything to implicate him in any way."

Sanders, asked, "Pete tells me that Janie had called him and needed to talk about something she had learned at Sneed, Weeks and King. He said that was why they went to the Playhouse together. They planned to talk about it after the play. Did you find out anything about this?"

"No," was all Stan could say.

Beginning his report, Sanders said, "As you know, I have been working with the police and they are ready to say out loud that they believe the shooting was a contract shooting. They believe the shooter was a young attractive woman from out of town who had been brought in for this job. They also think the shooter must have left town in a 2011 silver Lexus. That is all they know but they are concerned that, if Pete was the target, the shooter might try again."

"Sanders, please don't tell me that, I'm already worried to death," said Sue.

"What about this thing with Al and Sally?" asked Sam.

"That's where I have been spending most of my time. I am not sure how it all ties together but I believe it is somehow connected to the shooting. What I can tell you is that Al and Sally have seen the baggage handlers stealing merchandise from the baggage, storing it and then moving it to a warehouse where it is loaded into an eighteen wheeler to transport somewhere. Pete is working on an undercover case that sounds something like it could fit in with all this."

The others had several question about Al, Sally and the baggage handlers that Sanders was not able to answer because he had promised Pete that he would not tell the family about Operation Delta Pride.

+++++

Vic and Woodie had made their deliveries and Mike had collected the money. Now Mike was on the phone with his Dad. Leon Wesson asked, "How was the trip and do you have the money?"

"The trip was alright and yes, I do have the money---all $1,250,000 of it."

"If the trip was just alright, what happened?"

"We only had one scary time. Around Champaign, IL a trooper pulled Vic over and inspected his paperwork and truck. However, after about twenty minutes he sent Vic on his way without opening the truck's back doors. By the way, where do the guys go to pick up their load for the return trip to Memphis?"

"Tell Vic to call Mario Moore at 312-872-8904 and he will set it up for both trucks and you need to head this way. When you're on your way, call Joe Cole and find out where and when in Memphis he wants you to drop off the money."

"Sounds good to me. I'm kinda sleepy but I plan to deliver the money before I take a nap."

"Make sure you do," said Leon before he closed his phone. He couldn't help being nervous until the whole trip was done and the money was secure.

+++++

At straight up 8:00 a.m. Pete heard the doorbell and then heard Alice yell out, "Pete, I'm here."

"Come on in," yelled Pete, as he continued reading his morning paper.

Seeing that Pete had set up an office in the 'living room' area, Alice asked, "Okay, where do I start?"

"Last night, by threatening to do it myself, I was able to get Dad to move some things around. He got you a desk and file set up, along with a computer and phone. Actually, he got me a new office set up and I gave you mine. So, your office is in the bedroom where we talked yesterday and my office will be in here. I need you to start by moving the stuff in your desk to my new desk. Keep the files in your office. I will only need a small file box on my desk."

Alice was a fast worker and in two hours most everything had been set up in both offices and it was time for Pete to explain to Alice what she would be doing. Sitting at his desk, with Alice setting across from him, he noticed again how attractive she was. Then he said, "Alice, we are working on two cases only. One case has to do with Janie's murder and the attempted murder on yours truly. Most of the people you will be talking to on this case are members of the Dover Detective Agency and the Memphis Police Department." Pete stopped and gave Alice time to ask any questions she may have.

"The second case is highly confidential. You are not to talk about this case with anyone but me. It involves what the Justice Department has named 'Operation Delta Pride'. Its mission is to discover the leaders of a drug trafficking ring that operates from Memphis to Helena. Sanders, Al and Sally are three people you will get to know because they are involved in this investigation. Ruby is an undercover agent in Helena who will be calling from time to time. To talk about this case outside this office could get her killed. "

"I don't know enough to ask questions," said Alice.

"I understand that, so we'll just take it a day at a time. If you need to know anything just ask."

+++++

In Atlanta, Carol's private cell phone rang and the caller said, "Pete has just moved home to continue his recovery. I understand he will not be able to come back to work at the Department of Justice office for about a month. However, he will be doing some work at home. Let's give it about a week, and then I want you to take him out."

"Just tell me where and when and I'll be there," said Carol.

"I'll call you and Carol; I don't want you to miss this time. It is time for him to die," the caller said, as he hung up his phone.

After Carol got off the phone, she began to make plans to make a quick trip to Memphis. She wanted to look the situation over. There couldn't be another screw up.

+++++

Alice was about to leave for the day and had gone into Pete's office to say goodbye for the day when Pete asked her, "How is the apartment hunting going?"

"I have two to look at tonight. I really don't like the location but the price is right."

Pete had a good day with Alice. He felt she was going to be just what he needed to feel like he was accomplishing something. He wondered if, in the world today, he could ask her if she wanted to rent a room from him. She could help him out with his disability problems instead of paying rent. But could he keep it strictly business? Would he even want to keep it strictly business? Instead of asking her, he said, "I'll see you in the morning."

Chapter Eleven

Helena
The Pot
June 20

Mike had delivered the money in the way Joe Cole had told him. He had met an attorney in an I-55 rest stop just inside the Mississippi line. He had no idea what happened to it after he handed it over to the attorney but that was not his problem. That was Joe Cole's problem. He was much more interested in Ruby Shipman.

Calling Ruby he got her voicemail, "Leave your name and number and I'll get back to you."

"This is Mike and you have my number. I should be back in Helena in about an hour and wanted to see you. Please call."

Next, Mike called his dad, "Dad, just wanted to let you know I should be back in time for lunch at the Island. Can you meet me?"

"Sounds good to me. We need to talk about your next project. See you then."

Mike was not too excited about Dad's "next project" but he knew he needed to get ready. His dad had told him they needed to move the drugs they had stored. That meant he needed to get police officers lined to help get the drugs to the dealers in the various towns within a couple hundred miles. Lucky for him, Joe had the personnel in place. His job would be to let everyone know when and then oversee delivery.

When Mike's phone rang again, Ruby said, "Why don't you come by the dealership when you get in town?"

"Sounds like a plan to me. However, I can't stay long because I have to meet Dad at the Island Café at noon. Be there in twenty minutes."

+++++

Exactly twenty minutes later, Mike pulled his truck into the Ford dealership. Ruby was involved with a customer but gave Mike a wave and yelled, "I'll be right with you."

Mike waved to Ruby as he parked his truck. However, it was so hot that he left his motor and air conditioner running as he walked to the showroom.

"I wanted to see you and tell you how sorry I am for the way our date ended the other night," Ruby said as she entered the showroom.

"Does that mean you would be willing to make up for it?"

"I would. What did you have in mind?"

"I just got back from a trip and I have to meet Dad for lunch, but I wondered, if you were up to it, maybe we could have dinner and maybe even go dancing."

"If that is an invitation, I would love to. I get off at 6:00 and could be ready by 7:00 if that works with you."

"I'll pick you up at 7:00. And, he said teasingly, I plan to limit the amount you drink tonight."

Ruby's face turned red as they agreed to the date and Mike told her he had to leave to meet his dad for lunch.

+++++

Alice rang the bell as she opened the front door of Pete's apartment. "I'm here," she yelled as she made her way to her office.

"Come to my office, there are some things I want to talk about," replied Pete.

Alice put her purse on her desk and made her way to Pete's office. "What do you have on your mind?" she asked as she sat down in front of his desk.

"First, tell me about your apartment hunting. Did you find anything you liked?"

Alice went into a longwinded story about the two apartments. It amounted to---one was in need of some major repair which the landlord was unwilling to do and the second one was in one of roughest neighborhoods in Memphis. She finished the longwinded story with, "so, you see, it was just a waste of time. I'd live in a tent in your backyard before I would live in either one."

"When do you have to move?"

"Let's see, this is Wednesday, June 20. I have to be out before Monday, June 25. So I have four days to find an apartment and get moved."

There it was. Pete had been thinking about it all night. He had decided to ask Alice to move in with him. That would give her a month to find her own apartment and it would give him some help during his recovery. He still wasn't sure he could keep it strictly business. But he had decided it was worth the effort.

"Well, I've been thinking about your problem and my problem and I have an idea that I want to run by you. You know I have a third bedroom, which has its own bath, and I---well---I was just wondering if you would like to move in here while you look for an apartment. That would give you another month to find a suitable apartment and it would give me some help during my recovery."

Alice looked stunned. Never in a million years would she have expected it to be this easy. She liked Pete and it was her plan to move in with him. It would make everything she had to do so much easier. However, she didn't want to appear too eager. After all, she would be sleeping in the room next to him. He would see her in the mornings before she had "made herself beautiful".

"I can see some advantages for both of us in this kind of arrangement but I have to admit, I'm a little uncomfortable with the idea of living with you. I, also, wonder what you mean by giving you some help during your recovery."

Pete replied, "To be honest, I was a little uncomfortable with the idea at first, but after thinking about it for a couple of days I believe it could work. As to helping me during my recovery, I really meant pitching in with the meals and other odds and ends. This could be a way for you to pay the rent. As you may know Mom hired a woman to come and do the housework."

+++++

Mike entered the Big Island Café in time to see Joe Cole sitting down with Frank Castle and his dad. Joining them, he gave the waitress his lunch order and said, "The trip went great, everything got delivered, we got our money and I am really glad to be home."

"Tell us about the trooper stopping Vic, that's got me worried," said Leon.

"When Vic first called me, it scared the hell out of me. But looking back there is nothing to worry about. The trooper pulled Vic over, checked his paper work and then checked the truck. After about thirty minutes, he sent him on his way. Never even asked to open the back doors."

Leon looked at Joe and asked, "Joe, what do you think?"

"Mike is probably right. However, just to play it safe, it might be smart to take Vic's truck off the road for a while."

Mike really didn't want to do that. That was the best truck they had and he felt there was no reason to pull it from the road. However, he knew when it came to matters of the law, Joe had the last word and there was no use arguing the point.

Changing the subject, Mike asked his dad, "Before I left for the trip north, you said we needed to talk about getting the drugs delivered. What do you have in mind?"

"I think we have enough processed for three loads. We need to take a load to Little Rock and one to Fayetteville. Then, one would go to the same place that you and Vic made the pick up in Memphis. The three loads should bring us $1,200,000. Do you want to deliver all three loads or would you rather split it up with Vic and Woodie?"

"What are you planning for me to use to deliver the stuff?"

"I thought, if we could get everything in the tires on the ground and the special box we made to fit between the spare tire and the truck bed, you could take your truck. After all, a pickup is the most common vehicle on the road."

"Then, you want me to deliver all three loads?"

"I think so. I thought you might go to Memphis tomorrow, Little Rock on the 26th and Fayetteville on the 28th. How do you feel about it?"

"I believe that would work. I might even ask Ruby to ride to Fayetteville."

"I don't see anything wrong with that. A couple might not attract as much attention as a single male. Just make sure you drop her off at the motel or a mall before you make your drop. Bring your truck out early in the morning and we'll load her up."

Things around the lunch table moved on to much less serious things. However, before he left, Mike said, "Dad, I've got a date with Ruby tonight and I plan for it to be a long night. What if I leave my truck now so it can be loaded? I'll be here by noon tomorrow."

"No problem. But what are you going to drive?"

"I was thinking about taking yours." Leon drove a new Cadillac XTS and Mike had been dying to drive it ever since Leon brought it home.

"I can deal with that. I've got the new worn off now."

Chapter Twelve

Memphis
Relationships
June 20

    Mike had call Ruby around 3:00 p.m. to discuss plans for their date. He wanted everything to be perfect. "Let me tell you what I have planned," Mike said. "A buddy of mine tells me we should to go to the Rum Boogie Café which is on Beale Street. He and his wife went there and he says it is not a real dressy place but they had a lot of fun. I plan to wear jeans. They had a wonderful meal and sat and drank and listened to this fabulous jazz group. I checked and the same group is still there. There is a black guy that is great, and this long haired girl. He says it was very romantic and a lot of fun. What do you think?"
    Ruby could tell he had put some time in planning the evening. There was no way she could ever tell him she had spent most of her life in New Orleans and had heard some of the best jazz groups. Instead she said, "Sounds like a wonderful evening. I love listening to good jazz and just knowing that you planned the evening will make it special."

Ruby couldn't help herself, she liked this man and she knew he was expecting tonight to be the night that she gave him what he had been wanting. To be honest with herself, "She wanted it, too."

+++++

Alice was about to leave for the day as she took two files into Pete's office. Sitting down, she said, "I've been thinking all day about what you said this morning. If you're serious, I will consider it. If I could do some extra work for my rent, I could save a little and that would help me when it was time to rent an apartment. However, I do have one major problem."

"I've found most problems can be solved if you are just honest and talk about it. So, what's the problem?"

"Remember you asked for it, so, I'm just going to blurt it out. I'm attracted to you. If I wasn't working for you I would be doing everything possible to get you to take me out socially. Therefore, if we are living in the same apartment, if I am sleeping in the room next to yours---there is no way in hell I can keep this on a 'strictly business' relationship."

Trying to get over the shock of what Alice had said, he thought, "If I wasn't confined to this apartment, I would invite her out for drinks so we could talk this over. I've always found problems like this can often be solved over a nice dinner, a little wine and maybe even some dancing." However, he WAS confined to the apartment. He continued his thoughts with, "Now, what was he to do?"

Pete's thoughts were interrupted when the phone rang. "Pete, this is Ruby, you got a minute?"

"Sure," replied Pete. It was Ruby, the undercover FBI agent in Helena. Alice left Pete's office because she knew that Pete would prefer that she not overhear the phone conversation.

Ruby told Pete that Mike had returned from a "trip up north" today and had asked her for a date tonight. "Mike said we will be going to a place called Rum Boogie Café which is on Beale Street. I believe we will be staying over in Memphis. What do you know about the Rum Boogie Café?'

Pete told her essentially the same thing that she had heard from Mike and then he asked, "What have you learned about this 'trip up north'?"

"Things have been really quiet here and since Mike just got back in town, I don't have anything new to report. I just wanted you to know about my date with Mike. I'll get back with you as soon as I can."

Pete knew Alice had gone back to her office. For Pete, this meant she did not want to leave the house before they finished their conversation. The question was still there, "What should he say or do?"

Alice heard Pete hang up the phone and decided to give Pete a minute before going back to his office. Then she heard him call out, "Alice, we need to finish our conversation."

Alice entered the room very shyly; afraid of what Pete might have to say. As she sat down she said, "I shouldn't have told you how attracted to you I am. I was simply trying to be honest and maybe I was too honest. I'm sorry."

"I'll admit that I was shocked to hear what you put into words but I must also admit that I have been dealing with the same issue. Now that this out in the open and we know it is a mutual issue, all we can do is deal with it."

"How do we deal with it?"

"My feeling is that we move forward with your move into this apartment and then take it a day at a time."

"Pete, you and I both know what is going to happen if we simply let nature take it course. However, I'm willing if you are."

After the agreement was made and Alice had left the apartment, Pete continued to put a lot of thought into the question, "What have I got myself into?" He also knew that it wouldn't take long to find out because she was moving in---in the morning.

+++++

Carol had been sitting in her Lexus watching Pete's apartment for hours when her phone rang. It was her employer. He said, "It's time to get it done. He is back in his own apartment. Tomorrow night would be a good time."

"That will work. I'm in Memphis watching his house even as we speak. It will be no problem to have everything set up by then." Carol heard her phone go dead as her employer hung up. She was glad she had been in Memphis all day. She had gotten the feel of Pete's part of town even if there had not been much activity around his apartment. A young attractive woman going into the apartment at 8:00 a.m. was the only thing she had seen. The woman could have left without Carol seeing her, but she didn't think so.

She began to think of everything that needed to be done before the hit. She would need to drive back to Atlanta and pick up her tools. It wouldn't be a problem to get the car exchange set up. She made the phone call and it was done. She had decided to leave the Lexus in Atlanta and drive her new blue Cadillac CTS-V Coupe. It would have to be a quick trip to Atlanta. She didn't have a lot of time and she had to get some sleep. It was important that she be rested for the hit.

Her thoughts were interrupted when the door of Pete's apartment opened and the woman, who went in at 8:00 a.m., came out. She looked happy. There was an air of excitement in the way she walked. Since it was just a little after 4:00 p.m., Carol figured she must have been working. Maybe she was the maid or a caretaker. In any case, it was good to know she got off at 4:00. Looking at her watch again, she decided she had better get on the road.

+++++

Mike picked Ruby up at 7:00 p.m. driving his Dad's Cadillac XTS. "Where is your truck? I wore my jeans so I could get in and out of the truck," said Ruby.

"I'd rather drive the truck but Dad needed to borrow it. Besides, I wanted to impress you with the Cadillac." The conversation on the way to Memphis was light with a lot of teasing coming from both them. It was a good start to the night which held high expectations for both of them.

Rum Boogie Café was everything it had been advertised to be. The food was good and even Ruby had to admit the jazz group was as good as she would have heard in New Orleans. In fact, she had heard the group while she was living in New Orleans. There was no doubt about it, romance was in the air.

About mid-way through the evening, Mike began to talk about the traveling he was about to do. "I have trips to Memphis, Little Rock and Fayetteville coming up, so I'm going to be on the road a lot."

"I've never been to Fayetteville. What kind of place is it? All I know is that it is the home of the U of A Razorbacks."

"That just fits nicely into my plans cause I was planning to ask you to go with me on that trip."

"Would I be in the way? What are you going to be doing after you get there?"

Mike replied, "No, you would not be in the way. I have a meeting that will last about an hour. I could let you sleep in while I'm in my meeting. You probably will never miss me."

"My meeting is on Thursday, June 28th. That means I will need to leave on the 27th.

"I'll have to check to see if I can get off, but I would love to go with you."

With the trip settled, things got kind of quiet as Mike and Ruby listened to the music. Mike teased Ruby about not drinking too much and Ruby surprised him by saying, "If you're so interested in how much I'm drinking, then maybe we need to go. Where do you have the reservations?"

"Hotel Peabody."

"Then, what are we waiting for---let's go," said Ruby.

+++++

Al and Sally had been seeing a lot of each other. Most of the time, it had been the issue with the baggage handlers that had brought them together. Al would stay at the airport after he got off from Air Traffic Control and wait for Sally's plane to land. While he was waiting, he watched the baggage handlers as they continued to make off with luggage that never got delivered to the proper owners. At the rate they were going, they would need to move the stuff soon.

Al was watching Sally walk toward their table, when he realized his heart was beating a little faster. He had not realized how serious his feelings for her had become. It seemed he couldn't help thinking of her blue eyes and wonderful body. Tonight she looked more beautiful than ever.

"What's happening?" Sally asked as she approached Al.

Al didn't want to tell her what he had been thinking about, instead he said, "I've been watching for almost two hours and haven't seen a thing. To be honest, I have been kind of bored. However, now that your plane has landed things have really picked up."

Al had picked up some food for a sack lunch---nothing special, just burgers, fries and a Pepsi. However, they were enjoying it while they watched another repeat performance of Victor and the other baggage handlers. As before, the handlers took the last load from the Southwest plane and instead of taking it to baggage area in the airport, they took it to the bank or "safe place" in the Memphis airport. Al and Sally had the details of the operation and, with Pete and Sanders help, were reporting everything they had learned to the Justice Department.

However, something else was happening. Early on, Al had noticed how attractive Sally was but now she was becoming important to him because of who she was. With a cheeseburger in one hand and a Pepsi in the other hand, Al looked Sally in the eye and said, "I really didn't mean for this to happen and to be honest I don't know when it did, but I think I am falling in love with you."

Sally knocked the Pepsi out of his hand as she moved around the table, almost sat in his lap and said, "Me, too! So what do we do about it now?"

"Mom may kill me but I think its time we moved in together," said Al. "I also think, since the baggage handlers have completed their work, its time for us to leave. How about coming to my apartment and spending the rest of the night with me."

"Let me throw these leftovers away and then I'm ready." It would not be the first time Sally had gone to bed with Al but as a confirmation of their decision, it would be the most meaningful.

Chapter Thirteen

Memphis
Another Shooting
June 21

    Alice had been up since 4:30 a.m. trying to get everything packed that she would need. She and Pete had decided she would only bring what she would need today and then on Saturday they would enlist some of the Dover men to help her move everything else. However, since Alice lived in a furnished apartment, there would not be a lot to move.
    Alice unlocked the front door of Pete's apartment, rang the bell and yelled, "Pete, it's me," as she walked into the apartment. She had a suitcase in each hand and had left four more on the front steps.
    Pete saw her as she was walking toward her new bedroom. "I'm glad you made it. You know I would like to help carry in your stuff, but I can't. I promise I'll make it up to you someday."
    "Don't worry about it. It's really no problem. I'll have it all in and be ready to work in thirty minutes. I'll wait until I get off at 4:00 p.m. to put everything away."
+++++

Mike had made good time. He was a little early. He had pulled up in front of the warehouse at 4689 Brooks Road at 2:00 p.m. and was not due until 2:30. The overhead doors were still locked, so he pulled in, left the motor running to keep the air cold, leaned his seat back and smiled as he relived the night he had spent with Ruby.

Mike had not meant to go to sleep but the next thing he knew Daniel was taping on his door glass. Daniel was the same person he had met the other day when they loaded Vic's eighteen wheeler. Lowering the window, he said, "Sorry about that, I had a long night and was catching up on my sleep."

"That's okay, pull your truck in and we'll get this job done."

Mike pulled in his truck and two men went to work breaking down the tires so they could get to the Marijuana. After weighing the marijuana, they found Mike had brought 150 pounds broken down in dime and quarter bags. For that, Mike had been handed a briefcase filled with $450,000. After he counted the money, it was put in the special box which was located between the spare tire and the bed of the truck. The plan was for it to stay there until he got back to Big Island and the Pawn Shop.

As soon as Mike crossed the Tennessee/Mississippi state line, he dialed his phone. "Dad, it's done. I made the delivery, I got the money and I'm headed home."

"Good job, son. I'll see you in about ninety minutes."

What Mike didn't know was that the FBI had been watching. In fact, they had been watching his truck ever since June 16th when Al and Sally had seen his truck at the same warehouse. They had even gotten a court order and put cameras inside the warehouse on Brooks Road to keep watch when they were not there. Today, they had a solid case against

Mike for drug trafficking, however, on the advice of Pete, justice had decided they were going after the very top of the crime ring. It had been accepted that this was going to take some time and that it was important to take the time to do the investigation correctly.

+++++

Carol had arrived in Memphis before dark and had taken up her surveillance of Pete's apartment. It was well after 4:00 p.m., so she had every reason to believe Pete was alone. Even if the woman who had been there all day yesterday had come back today, surely she was gone by now. Carol had everything prepared. The security system would be disarmed and the door would be easily opened. Carol wanted to wait until 1:00 a.m. before she acted. All she could do now was watch and wait.

Inside the apartment, Pete was finishing up some paper work on his desk while Alice had been putting her room into some sort of order. Sue, Pete's mother, had brought in food for lunch and there were plenty of leftovers for their evening meal.

As they sat down at the kitchen table, Pete began the conversation by saying, "I heard a lot of moving around in your room. Do you have everything put away?"

"It's coming together. When I finish up in the bathroom, I'm done for the day."

The rest of the conversation centered on Pete's job. They discussed the lack of progress. Every lead seemed to lead nowhere. There was a lot of suspicion that someone at Pete's old law firm was somehow involved but there was no evidence. Sanders felt sure that Operation Delta Pride was linked to the shooting, but again, there was no evidence.

However, progress was being made in Operation Delta Pride. They now had evidence on some of the "little people" in the drug trafficking. Pete felt that the "little people" would lead them to the leaders. They just had to be patient. Ruby had told Pete the next deliveries would be Little Rock on June 26th and Fayetteville on the 28th and that she would be going to Fayetteville with Mike.

Alice cleaned the kitchen, told Pete (who was at his desk) goodnight and went to her room to finish some loose ends before going to bed. It had been a long day. By 10:00 p.m. both of them were sound asleep.

+++++

Alice was suddenly wide awake. "But why?" she wondered. There had been a noise coming from somewhere near the back door. She lay very still, listening. Then, she heard it again, however, this time she knew it was coming from inside the apartment. "Someone is in the apartment," she thought. If it were Pete moving around, he would have turned on the lights.

"Okay, Alice, it is time for you to earn your money," she thought as she took her .40 caliber Glock 23 out of the headboard. Silently, she got out of bed and walked to her door which had been left open. Standing in her doorway, she listened for other sounds. She could hear Pete breathing hard as he slept. Then, she heard another noise which sounded like someone was coming from the kitchen through Pete's office. Pete had a night light in the kitchen which provided just enough light to see shadows.

From her doorway, Alice was looking down the hall that anyone would have to cross to get to Pete's room. She could feel it, someone was moving in Pete's office. Then, she could see him as he stepped from the office into the hall. The shadow she saw looked very small, almost like a child.

However, she could also see a hand with a gun in it. Alice called out, "Drop the weapon! Get your hands up!"

The shadow turned and fired his weapon, barely missing Alice. Alice returned fire and the shadow fell to the floor. Alice turned the hall light on and walked toward the shooter. She kicked the weapon from the shooter's hand noticing it was a 45 ACP equipped with a silencer. Pete yelled, "What the hell is going on?"

"Pete, call 911. I've just shot an intruder. I don't know if he is still alive. I'm checking for a pulse now."

As she examined the shooter, she learned it was a woman and she did have a weak pulse. "Pete, tell them to hurry, she is still alive."

However, Pete had already hung up the phone, so he said, "They said they would be here as soon as possible. They were also sending the police. We had better get something on before they get here and we might need to talk." Pete checked the shooter to be sure she was hurt too bad to bother either of them.

In all the excitement Alice had forgotten she had been sleeping in the nude. "Sorry about that," she said as she made her way to her bedroom.

Alice joined Pete in his office. He said, "Now that we are both presentable, you need to tell me what happened and how it happened. Who is this woman and how did you know she was in the house? And what are you doing with a handgun under you pillow?"

"I'm a very light sleeper. I guess that it woke me when she opened the back door. I heard something; I really didn't know what it was. When I heard it the second time I had the feeling that someone was in the house besides the two of us. That's when I got my Glock which I had put in the headboard of my bed. With my weapon in my hand, I walked to my door which I had left open. Finally, I could see her shadow as she stepped into the hall. When I saw her weapon, I yelled for her to drop the gun but instead she turned toward me and fired. I returned fire and she went down. You know the rest."

"You didn't tell me what you were doing with a weapon in the headboard of your bed and where did you learn to shoot like that?"

Before Alice could answer, the doorbell was ringing. Alice hurried to open it and led the EMTs to the hall where the shooter was laying. The EMTs tried to stabilize her before moving her to their ambulance. She was still alive when they left for the hospital.

As the EMTs were leaving for the hospital, the police were coming up the sidewalk. Alice introduced herself, invited them in and introduced them to Pete. But as luck would have it the police team was Officer Dick Goodman and Officer Joe Dugan. Goodman said, "We already know Mr. Dover. We were the officers called to the scene about two weeks ago when he was shot and Janie Albert was killed. Mr. Dover, how are you tonight?"

"Thanks to Alice here, I'm much better than I was the last time. She kept the shooter from getting to my room and I will be forever grateful to her. I didn't know what was happening until it was over. Do you mind if I call my parents before they hear about the shooting on their scanner?"

"Go right ahead," said Dugan. "Meanwhile, I would like take a look at the crime scene." Alice showed the officers through the house, pointing out who was in which bedroom. She also took them through Pete's office, kitchen and on to the back door which was still open giving evidence that the shooter entered the house through the back door.

"I tried to tell Mom and Dad that I was alright and they did not need to come over, but they will be here in a few minutes," said Pete.

The two officers and Pete and Alice found a place to sit in Pete's converted office. Goodman said, "I'd like to get your statements before anyone gets here. Alice, since you were the one most involved, I would like to start with you."

Alice was glad she had just told Pete what had happened. It provided a kind of practice run for the real thing with the police.

After completing her statement, Dugan asked the same question that Pete had. "What were you doing with a weapon in the headboard of your bed?"

At this point Alice felt it best to tell a half truth. "I just moved my stuff in and had not found a home for my Glock.

The officers turned to Pete for his statement which picked up after the shooting started. "We taped your statements tonight. I'll get them typed up and bring them by for you to sign tomorrow," said Officer Goodman as he and his partner were getting up to leave.

Sue was running up the front steps and almost knocked Officer Goodman down as he was coming out the front door. Andy stopped to talk with the police as Sue rushed into the apartment to make sure Pete was alright. Pete was still setting in his temporary office while Alice was seeing the officers out. "Son, are you okay? They didn't hurt you did they?"

"Mom, I'm fine and there was not a 'they', there was just one very small woman and she is on the way to the hospital. However, you do need to thank Alice. If it had not been for her, I might not be alive."

Alice had said good-bye to the police and was talking to Andy as she closed the front door. The two of them walked into the office where Sue simply could not break herself away from Pete. "Now, Sue, let Pete tell us what happened," Andy said as he looked at Pete.

Pete said, "Let Alice tell you, I slept through most of it." So, for the third time in an hour, Alice told her story.

After she finished her story, Andy asked the same question. "What were you doing with a weapon in the headboard of your bed and where did you learn to shoot like that?"

This time Alice told another half truth. She said, "My family was into guns and shooting. We went to the range as often as we could. My favorite weapon was the .40 caliber Glock 23. For my eighteenth birthday, Dad bought me my very own."

"And I, for one, am glad he did," said Pete.

Chapter Fourteen

Memphis
Regrouping
June 22

"Carol is unconscious in ICU at Baptist East Hospital and she must not be allowed to wake up. You must take care of it," the caller said.

"I'll get it done."

+++++

After everyone had left Pete's apartment there were some tender moments between Pete and Alice. "I'm just glad you decided to move in yesterday. Apparently the shooter thought I was alone. And I'm glad you're a light sleeper. And I'm glad you had a weapon and knew how to use it."

"Me too. But Pete there is something I need to tell you."

"Go ahead."

Alice had no idea how Pete was going to react to what she had to say, but she owed it to him to be honest. "I don't know how to say it, so, be patient with me. You see, I'm not just your helper while you're confined to this apartment."

Pete was becoming impatient, "You're stalling, get on with it."

"Okay, here it is, and I know I shouldn't tell you this, but I was sent here by US Attorney, Debra Witcher, to protect you. She was afraid there would be another attempt on your life. I am actually an undercover FBI agent."

The room became silent. Alice could see the emotion in Pete's face. With a lot of anger in his voice, she heard him say, "So that's why you had a weapon in the headboard of your bed---that's how you learned to shoot."

"Yes," was all she could say.

"You manipulated me into asking you to move in with me. You made me think it was my idea."

Again, all she could say was, "yes."

"I'll have to say you're very good at your job." Without another word, Pete got up and went to his room.

+++++

When Andy got to the hospital at 7:30 a.m., he found a police officer guarding Carol's ICU room which told him Carol was still alive. The police officer told him he didn't know her condition, but that she had just gotten in her room. She had been in surgery most of the night.

Andy had called Sanders while he was on the way to the hospital. He asked to meet with him at the ICU waiting room because he needed to talk. Andy had assured Sanders that everyone in the family was okay. Sitting there waiting for Sanders made Andy really feel funny. Just two weeks ago he had been here, praying and waiting to see if Pete was going to live. Now, the person who had killed Janie and almost killed Pete was in the same situation.

Andy's phone rang, and he answered it with, "Good morning, Pete, how are you feeling this morning?"

"Maybe a little better, but it was a long night and I've been doing a lot of thinking. There are some things I need to tell all of you, and I was wondering if you could call a meeting of the Dover Detective Agency for noon today. I could call out for pizza if you could meet at my apartment."

"I could do that, but why?"

"I would rather wait and tell everybody at the same time."

Andy wasn't too happy with that answer, but he said, "I'll set it up. If you don't hear back from me, you know it's a go."

Even before he closed his phone, Andy saw Sanders walking into the waiting room with a "What's going on?" look on his face, and that was exactly what he asked when he sat down beside Andy.

"Andy, what is going on?"

"Get comfortable, it's a long story." Then, Andy laid out the shooting that had taken place just six hours before.

"Hells, bells, why didn't you call me?"

"Pete and Alice were alright. We decided there was nothing you could do until this morning, so we let you sleep."

"Who is the shooter? Is she the same one who tried to kill Pete two weeks ago?"

"One question at a time, please. We don't know who she is. There was no ID found on her. We believe she is the same person. She fits the description that was given by the Wal-Mart clerk."

"Sanders, Pete just called and wanted me to call a meeting at noon at his apartment. Can you be there? He's serving pizza."

"Sure, I'll be there."

Andy continued, "I was wondering if you had any idea what he wanted to tell all of us."

Sanders figured Pete was ready to talk about Operation Delta Pride. "I might, but Pete swore me to secrecy. I'd rather he told us all together."

After talking to the doctors about the shooter's condition and setting up the meeting, Andy and Sanders left the hospital.

+++++

Blurry eyed, Alice walked into the kitchen to find Pete drinking coffee. The gown she was wearing left little to the imagination. He was wide awake and looked as though he had already had a whole pot of coffee. "You want some breakfast?" she asked.

God, she was beautiful when she was blurry eyed, didn't have on a bra and her hair was uncombed. "Not right now, first we need to talk."

Alice got a cup from the cabinet, poured it full and sat down at the table. Since she had no idea what Pete wanted to talk about she said, "Okay, let me have it."

"Unless you're suggesting that we go to bed together, I don't want to 'let you have it'. I want to apologize for being an ass last night. You saved my life and I treated you like dirt. I don't even know why I was mad at you. All I know for sure is that I would like a chance to start over with you."

Alice looked at him and said, "An attempt had just been made on your life. You're allowed to be upset."

"You had just shot someone. I should have been comforting you. Will you every forgive me?"

There were tears in Alice's eyes as she said, "Of course I will." Then she walked around the table, put her arms around Pete and kissed him on the lips. Pete responded in the same way any red blooded man would. He pulled her down in his lap, held her tight and returned her kiss. After a while, he said,

"We'd better stop this now or we may start something we can't stop."

"I know, so, maybe I'd better change the subject. Have you heard how the shooter is this morning?"

"I talked to Dad a while ago. He was at the hospital checking on her. He said she had made it through the surgery but was still very critical and was expected to be unconscious for several days."

"When I first saw her, I thought she was a child. She looked so small. In spite of what she was trying to do, I hope she lives."

Pete was still holding Alice and things had gotten really quiet. Alice moved to get more comfortable in Pete's lap and Pete realized he had his hand on her bare breast. "I didn't mean to do that. In fact, I didn't know what I was doing until you moved. You had better get up and I'll cook the breakfast this morning."

"You sure?" she answered.

Pete didn't know what she was asking. Did she mean, "Was I sure I wanted her to get up or was I sure I wanted to cook breakfast." To be honest with himself, he had to admit he didn't have the answer to either question, but he did begin to get up and start cooking breakfast.

Alice moved around the table, got her coffee and started to her room saying, "I think I'd better go to my room and get dressed. Yell, when you get it on the table."

+++++

The Dover Detective Agency had gathered in Pete's apartment. The apartment was a little small but Pete and Alice had spent the morning moving things around so everyone could gather in Pete's office. Everyone was there except Stan and Pat who were spending time at Gulf Shores with their friends,

Amy and Joe Appleton.

As usual, Andy called the meeting to order but told everyone this meeting had been called by Pete. "All of you know there was another attempt on Pete's life last night and I assume that has something to do with what Pete wants to talk about. Therefore, I'm turning the meeting over to him so he can tell us what he has on his mind."

Pete began, "You have no idea how glad I am to be here today. Without Alice, wait a minute, I'm not sure all of you have met Alice. Alice stand up. This is Alice. Without Alice, in all probability, I would not be here today. By standing between me and the shooter, she saved my life last night."

The whole clan said it together, "Thank you, Alice." And Alice's face turned red. Then, Pete told them that he had just found out that Alice was, in fact, an FBI agent sent here by his boss to protect him.

Pete went on to apologize to everyone because he had not been completely honest about his work. He told them about Operation Delta Pride and the undercover agent in Helena and how Sanders, Al and Sally, sort of accidentally, got involved. "With their help, we are beginning to close in on some of the players, but we want the team leaders. I believe someone involved in this drug trafficking is responsible for the attempts on my life."

Andy was critical of Pete for keeping this information from the family and Sue almost had a conniption fit because her son was involved in something so dangerous. She said, "I sent you to college so you could be safe in the courtroom convicting the bad guys."

After several other comments, Andy moved the meeting on with, "As shocking as this new information is, the real question becomes, what are we going to do with it?"

Gracie asked, "Pete, what do you need from us?"

"Well, Mom and I would prefer that there were no more attempts on my life. That means we need to find out who hired the shooter. I understand she is still unconscious, with a small chance of recovering. Someone needs to be there in case she wakes up. She may be our only lead to the person who is calling the shots."

"Hospital work is a woman's job," said Gracie. "What if Sue and I take care of it?"

Sue nodded that it would be okay with her, and Andy said, "Then it's settled. Sue and Gracie have the hospital duty. What else. Pete?"

"I've been thinking about the question of how the shooter got to my apartment. If she followed the same plan, there is an older car out there near my apartment. There would also be a newer car somewhere, possibly in some retail store's parking lot, that she planned to swap with the older car. If we could find either of these cars, we might be able to find some evidence that would lead us to the top man."

"That sounds like my job," said Andy.

Pete continued, "Sally and Al will continue to watch the baggage handlers and see if they can determine who is receiving their stolen items. I want Sanders to continue working with them." Pete told the group that he continued to suspect someone at his old law firm of Sneed, Weeks and King to be responsible for leadership in the drug trafficking. "I'm convinced Janie knew something about this, however with her death that information is lost. Sanders, will you check this out?"

"I'll be glad to. I had thought about focusing on that red pickup. Following it everywhere it goes to see what I can discover."

Pete responded, "That may come later. Right now the FBI and the undercover agent in Helena are doing a good job keeping me informed."

Sam said, "Right now I'm covered up with the McClintock case." He added jokingly, "Somebody in this family has to be making some money. However, if you need me, just call."

Chapter Fifteen

Jackson, Mississippi
Janie's Parents
June 23

Stan's cell phone rang in Gulf Shores, Alabama. "The caller said, "This is Carl Albert in Jackson, Mississippi, and I need to talk to you."

"Yes, I remember you well. How are you and Mrs. Albert doing? Pat and I think of you often."

"We are taking it a day at a time and are beginning to see some of the shock leave us. However, something happened this morning that I need to talk about with you."

"What happened?"

"My wife and I remember that you suggested Jamie might have seen or found something at her work that led to her death. We didn't really believe that to be the case. However, today we decided to try to put away some Janie's belongings, and well, you just need to see what we found."

"My wife and I are about four hours from your place. Could we meet you at 6:00 p.m.?"

"That would be good for us. We look forward to our meeting."

+++++

Andy had spent the morning walking through the neighborhood around Pete's apartment. He had listed five cars that he felt might be the shooter's second car. He was now trying to discover who owned the five cars. That is, he was until his phone rang. "Andy this is your dad. You got a minute to talk?"

"Sure, Dad. What's on your mind?"

"Your mom and I are having a great time at Gulf Shores, but this morning I got a call from Carl Albert."

"Who?"

"You know, Janie's dad. He found something in Janie's belongings that he feels might be important. He wouldn't tell me much. Instead, he wanted Pat and me to meet him in Jackson at 6:00 tonight. I wonder if you could meet us there."

"I'm not sure I can. There was another attempt made on Pete's life and Sue would kill me if I left town right now, but I could send Sanders."

"What do you mean? There was another attempt on Pete's life? Was he hurt? Is he in the hospital? Why didn't you call us?"

"Slow down, Dad. Pete's alright. This time it was the shooter that was hurt. Alice is working with Pete, and since her apartment is closing down, she is staying with Pete for a while. Since Alice is an FBI agent, she was able to shoot the intruder before she was able to get to Pete. The intruder is critical and unconscious in the hospital. We didn't think there was anything you could do and we didn't want to worry you, so we were waiting to call you."

Stan was not sure he liked being left out and he was sure Pat would raise the roof. He said, "We'll talk about this later. See if Sanders can meet us in Jackson and have him call us." Stan knew Sanders would tell him what really happened in this second shooting.

+++++

Sue had arrived at the hospital at 6:00 a.m. to relieve Gracie, who had spent the night. Gracie had told Sue everything had been quiet and the nurses seemed to think the shooter was better. However, she was still unconscious. After Gracie had left, Sue talked with the policeman who was guarding the shooter. He had assured her that no one was going to get past him.

The ICU room, where the shooter was, seemed to be very busy with doctors and nurses coming and going at all times. Sue was able to stop one doctor long enough to ask about the patient's condition. He said, "I didn't believe she would be alive today, but she is and she is stronger than she was yesterday. If she improves again tomorrow, she will have a good chance of making it. The fact that she is unconscious actually gives her a better chance."

+++++

Sanders knew Gracie would be asleep, so he sent her a text, "Honey," he wrote, "I figured you were asleep after working all night at the hospital and I didn't want to wake you. I just got a call from Andy and I have to go to Jackson, Mississippi and meet your dad. Janie's parents called Stan this morning and they have found something that they wanted him to see. Stan wants me there. I love you. Call me when you wake up."

Next, he called Pete. "Pete, have you talked with Andy? Do you have any idea what Janie's parent have found in Janie's belongings?

"Not really," said Pete. "But give me a call when you find out. I have always thought that whatever Janie intended to talk to me about was important. I'll be waiting for your call."

With those two calls out of the way, Sanders was on his way to Jackson. He would have to stop at a convenience store for something to eat. He had plenty of time, so this was one time he would not have to rush.

+++++

Frank Castle had suggested that Mike bring Ruby out to Big Island more often. It seemed that Mike was getting involved with her and if that was true, he wanted to get to know her better. Therefore, it was no surprise when Mike and Ruby walked into the Café for lunch.

Frank and Joe Cole were having lunch together. No one seemed to know where Leon was, so, Frank invited Mike and Ruby to join them. The food was good. The conversation, which was being led by Frank, was light and Frank seemed to be flirting with Ruby. She wasn't sure what to make of it, but she felt Frank's leg against her's several times. Ruby always had a good time; she gave back as good as she got. Joe had very little to say which reminded Ruby of the saying; "It's the quiet ones you have to watch."

"I understand you're from St. Louis. Tell me something about your life there," said Frank.

"I lived in St. Louis for twenty some years. In fact, I graduated from Soldan International Studies High School."

"I don't know that school."

"Well, let's see. It has a great band, basketball, football program, and there are lots of good looking boys. It is located on 918 N Union Blvd in St. Louis, MO. The school community has given it a rating of 5 out of 5 stars." Ruby felt like she was being given a test. She was just glad she had studied.

Ruby knew Mike had two trips to make next week. She was planning to go to Fayetteville on the 27th and 28th with him. However, she was surprised when Frank brought it up. "Mike," he said, "is everything set for your trips to Little Rock and Fayetteville?" Ruby wondered if he knew she was going to Fayetteville with him, but she didn't have to wonder long. "Mike tells me you have never been to Fayetteville. Make him show you around the University."

+++++

Andy had found two older cars with "junk yard" tags. One was a four door, 2004 Chevrolet Impala while the other was a 2005 Chrysler Town and Country. Andy called Captain Davis, told him what he had found and asked him to send out a detective to help determine if the shooter might have been driving one of the cars.

"Detectives Jerry Searcy and Mark Melton, who are assigned to Pete's case, are here in my office. They will be right there." Within twenty minutes the detectives were parking their car next to Andy's.

"What do we have?" Melton asked.

"I have two cars that have license plates that belong on other cars. This leads me to believe that one of the cars could have been used by the shooter. Neither of the cars has been moved since the shooting. The Chrysler has lots of junk in it. This Chevrolet is clean. I can't see a thing left in it. If I had to guess, I would say she was driving the Chevrolet."

Searcy said, "And I would agree with you. Since the tags don't belong on this car, we have the right to open the car and search it. Let's see what we can find, just try not to touch anything."

All three of the men put on gloves and Melton open the driver's door with his slim jim tool set. Sure enough the car was clean. Nothing was in it. Andy said, "Keep looking, there has to be something." Then he saw it. Crammed between the two bucket front seats was, what appeared to be, a woman's purse. Pulling out the purse, Andy took it to the hood of the car. With the detectives looking on, he poured the contents of the purse onto the car hood.

Detective Searcy took the wallet and begin to look through it while Andy and Melton looked at the purse contents. They found lipstick and other makeup, keys, tissue, condoms, tampons, change, and a cell phone with a dead battery. Searcy found $234.00, a visa debit card and a driver license in the wallet. The picture on the driver's license looked like the shooter. The driver license and debit card belonged to Carol Wooten, 6758 Cogbill Road, Atlanta, GA.

Searcy dialed information for Carol Wooten in Atlanta, GA. He heard the machine say, "The number is 470-691-4472." When he dialed the number, again he heard the machine. This time he heard a young woman say, "Please, leave your name and number and I'll get back to you."

Andy noticed the keys found in the purse did not belong to the Chevrolet. He was also sure they did not belong to the silver Lexus she had been seen getting into on the Wal-Mart parking lot. The key ring had a Cadillac emblem on it. There must be a Cadillac sitting empty on a parking lot somewhere in the city.

Searcy dialed Georgia DMV told them who he was and asked them to check for Carol Wooten at 6758 Cogbill Road, Atlanta. See what kind of cars she drives. Sure enough it was a 2011 silver Lexus LX and a 2012 blue Cadillac CTS-V Coupe. Somewhere out there in the city of Memphis was a 2012

Cadillac that was waiting for a driver who would not show up. Searcy called it in and put out an APB for the car.

+++++

Sanders had agreed to meet Stan and Pat at a Wendy's which was close to Mr. and Mrs. Carl Albert's home. When Sanders pulled his car into the space in front, Stan and Pat were nowhere in sight. He leaned his seat back, closed his eyes and got comfortable. However, it was not long before Stan and Pat were knocking on his door glass. "Let's go in, I need a Pepsi Max." said Stan.

As soon as they got their drinks and found a seat, Pat said, "Sanders, I want to know what happened to Pete and I want to know why you didn't call me."

"Pat, I couldn't; Pete is calling the shots on this case and he told us not to call you because there was nothing you could do. He is alright. The shooter never got close to him. Alice made sure of that."

"Who is Alice?"

Sanders realized Pat would never settle for the short version of what happened in Pete's apartment, so he told them the story as told by Pete in the meeting, including the fact that Alice is an FBI agent. He also told them he had just gotten a call from Andy who has discovered the shooter was a young woman named Carol Wooten, who lived at 6758 Cogbill Road, in Atlanta, GA. And, that it is assumed someone hired her to kill Pete.

As they were leaving Wendy's, Sanders felt he had been able to take some of the anger out of Pat. She still wasn't happy that they had been left out, but at least she understood that their motives were good. All Sanders knew for sure was that Andy and Pete owed him---big time.

+++++

Carl Albert was surprised to see three people walking toward their front door. He recognized Stan and Pat Dover. He had met them at Janie's funeral and he liked them. However, he had no idea who the other man was. He was a little uncomfortable sharing personal information, about his daughter, with someone he had not met.

By the time the doorbell rang, Mrs. Albert had joined her husband. Mrs. Albert invited her guests in and the introductions were made. She asked everyone to call her Julie and she met Sanders, who she learned was Stan and Pat's son in law. Everyone was invited back to the den where Julie had tea and snacks available.

With the small talk completed, Carl said, "As I told you over the phone, we had not felt like dealing with Janie's belongings until now and we were making good progress until yesterday. That's when we found it. I don't know if we would have even noticed it if Stan hadn't asked us, 'Do you know of any reason your daughter might have been killed?' Of course, at the time we told you no."

Pat was very sensitive to the feelings that Carl and Julie had for their daughter. She said, "Take your time. No one is in a hurry."

"Thank you for that, but we have decided how we want to handle this. We have made copies of everything we have found. We will be keeping a copy and we want to give you the originals. Julie and I are not sure what it all means and, at this time, we are not emotionally able to discuss it with you. We hope you can use this material to help discover who killed our Janie. We now believe that Janie may have been killed because of what she knew about a drug trafficking ring. After you have studied the material, feel free to call us or come back and ask questions about the contents."

Sanders had dealt with this kind of situation during his time with the FBI. He felt it best to do exactly as the Alberts had asked. So, as they were leaving the Albert's home, Sanders said to Stan and Pat, "We need to talk. Let's go back to Wendy's."

+++++

Gracie was at the hospital keeping watch on Carol. The doctor had told her she had improved slightly. She was in and out of consciousness. However, even though she followed Gracie with her eyes, she would not answer any of her questions. In fact, she was not speaking at all.

Meanwhile, Gracie went back to the waiting room to answer her cell phone. It was Sanders, "Hello honey, I'm on my way back to Memphis. It'll be around 10:00 p.m. before I get there. Will you still be at the hospital?"

"Unless something changes, I plan to be here until Sue gets here at 6:00 in the morning. Could you come by when you get back to town? I've been missing you, and you could bring me something to eat. By the way, what did you learn in Jackson?"

"Not anything yet. The Alberts gave us a briefcase full of material to study. Pat and Stan are coming back to Memphis and they plan to stay with Andy and Sue. They have the briefcase with them. Stan said he planned to make Pat drive while he looked through the material. The three of us will meet with Pete at 8:00 in the morning."

"That gives us time to have breakfast together before I go to bed."

"What about Carol? How is she doing?" asked Sanders.

"The doctors tell me she is better and I have seen her regain consciousness. She is in and out. I have tried to talk with her but she won't or can't answer. Hope I know more when you get here at 10:00. I love you.

Sanders said, "I love you more," as he closed his phone.

+++++

Chapter Sixteen

Memphis
Attempted Murder
June 24

  Andy, Sanders, Stan and Pete were gathered in Pete's apartment at 8:00 a.m. Since Stan had the briefcase he had received from Carl Albert, Sanders fully expected Stan to lay out, for the rest of them, what was in the briefcase. Instead, Stan had made copies of everything in the briefcase and gave each person around the table a set of the materials. He said, "I believe each of us needs to read this material before we discuss it. Therefore, I want to suggest that we take our copies to a quiet place and read and think about what we have. We could reconvene at 11:00 a.m."

  "That might work; however, I have just gotten word that the police have located the 2012 blue Cadillac CTS-V Coupe that they believe Carol was driving. I would feel better if Sanders was watching over their shoulder as they check out the car," replied Andy.

  "Then we could reconvene at 1:00 p.m.," said Stan. Everyone agreed to this timeline and took their box of material and left Pete's apartment.

When everyone was gone, Pete asked Alice to work with him on Janie's material.

+++++

Sue could see an improvement in Carol when she came to the hospital at 6:00 a.m. She had actually heard her say a few words; however Sue wasn't able to understand what she was trying to say. Sue kept an eye on Carol's room as the team of doctors and nurses continued to care for her.

Around noon, Sue noticed a woman dressed as a nurse or maybe even a doctor go into Carol's room. Sue had never seen the woman before and wondered why a new person had suddenly joined the medical team. Going to the door of Carol's room, Sue stood and watched as the person checked the tubes that were connected to Carol and the machines. Looking around, the nurse/doctor asked Sue, "Could I help you? Do you need something?"

Sue told her who she was and what she was doing there and then questioned the nurse/doctor as to her name and asked if she was a new person on the medical team. "I'm Doctor Myer and I was asked by the lead doctor on the team to take a look at this patient."

"Who is the lead doctor on the team?" asked Sue.

"I can't remember his name. Let me see, where did I put the request?" Doctor Myer said as she started toward the door.

Sue called the police, who was guarding the room, and just as he was getting up Doctor Myer knocked him down and she ran over him getting out of the ICU. By the time Sue was able to get through the door, she was gone. Officer Morris, the policeman who was guarding Carol, called for backup. At this time there was mass confusion going on in ICU.

By the time the other police arrived, it was discovered that there was no Doctor Myer who worked in this hospital and it soon became apparent that the woman (Dr. Myer) was here to murder Carol Wooten.

Four members of the medical team arrived to check on Carol. Sue knew each of the four medical team members and she watched as they made sure that no harm had been done to their patient. The hospital administrator called Sue aside and said, "We want to thank you for being alert and for saving her life."

"Yeah, I guess, I did that even after she tried to kill my son," Sue thought.

+++++

"I don't understand what is going on," the caller was angry. "Two attempts on Dover's life and he is still alive and now you can't even take care of an unconscious girl. You shouldn't make these kinds of mistakes. It'll bring us all down."

"I know, chief. It won't happen again."

"There is so much protection around the both of them; you can't get to either one now. It would be better to back off for the moment, however, keep an eye on Carol. You can't let her talk."

After he hung up his phone, the contractor was a worried man. Carol had been one of his best, and in two tries she had not done her job. The chief was right, "I can't even get an unconscious girl killed. My profession requires that I be dependable. My life depends on it."

Chapter Seventeen

Memphis
The Plan
June 24

Stan, Andy, Sanders, Pete and Alice gathered in Pete's temporary office. Pete said "Before we get started with our thoughts on Janie's material, we need to clear up one loose end. Sanders, what did you and the police find in Carol's Cadillac?"

Nothing much, the girl keeps a clean car. I did find another cell phone. This one had a dead battery too. The police have assured me that they will charge the batteries of both phones and give us a report on what they find. The police are checking for prints now and will also let us know if they find anything of value."

"Before we leave the issue of Carol, I want to make a trip to 6758 Cogbill Road in Atlanta and check out what her living conditions are like."

Andy looked around and got a nod from everyone. "Everyone seems to think that's a good idea. When would you leave?"

"I could be there in less than two hours if I take the jet. I need to run by the house and see Gracie but I could do that while they are getting the jet ready."

Andy said, "That sounds like a plan. As soon as we finish here, get on the road or in the air, as the case may be."

"Moving on, I have to tell you, I'm shocked by what I have been reading since you guys left. I've known Janie for two years and had no idea she was involved in any of this," said Pete.

"My surprise was that she wrote it all down. The chief, and we don't know who that is yet, must have found out she had set up a meeting with Pete and that's why they wanted her out of the way," replied Sanders.

Andy said, "This means that Janie must have been the target. Pete was shot because he was with Janie and they had no idea what he might know."

The material they had been reading included a journal which outlined Janie's involvement in a drug ring; the "plan" which laid out how everything worked; and emails that supported the two documents. The "plan" supplied a lot of information to Pete and the Department of Justice except a lot of it was in a kind of code.

Names were in short supply. For example, the head of the drug ring was simply known as "Chief". He or she was not given a name. Other code names included: director, superintendent and Indians. Much of the code left them guessing, however, Pete was sure the code name "Trio" had to do with the Helena operation and was the code name for Frank Castle, Joe Cole and Leon Wesson. Then again, it could have meant, Sneed, Weeks and King. Pete, Stan, Andy and Sanders still had a lot to figure out, but at least they now had a map or outline of the operation. They just had to put names to the points on the map.

When it came to the journal, Pete said, "I have reread this twice and I am convinced that Janie was coming to me to try to make a deal. I think she wanted out, wanted to turn 'states evidence' and maybe get into the witness protection program."

Alice, who had been silent up to that point, said, "If you read between the lines in the last part of the journal, that's what it sounds like to me. At least that is what I would want to think if Janie had been my daughter."

"I agree and I'd like to be the one to tell Mr. and Mrs. Carl Albert when the time comes," said Stan.

+++++

When everyone had left Pete's, he called Alice to come in and talk. He wanted to thank her for backing him up in front of his family when he was talking about Janie turning states evidence. "There was never any romance involved in our relationship but I thought a lot of her. I'm having a hard time believing any of it. I have this need to believe she was trying to do the right thing at the end. This could easily be wishful thinking on my part."

"I didn't know her so I don't have an opinion except for the journal. Based on the journal, I believe your right."

"Thanks. I also wanted to talk to you about the other morning."

"I don't know what you mean," said Alice.

"You're not going to make this easy for me are you?"

Alice looked so honest and so attractive, and said, "I still don't know what you mean?"

"I'm sorry I put my hand under your gown and fondled your breast the morning after I made such an ass of myself by accusing you of manipulating me into asking you to move in with me."

"Oh!" said Alice. "Do you wish you hadn't done it? "As I remember, you kissed me. Are you sorry for that too?"

"Yes, I'm sorry for that too. It was not very professional. I should have had more control than that."

"Didn't you enjoy it?" asked Alice with just a touch of a grin on her face.

Pete started to answer again when he saw it. He could barely make it out but it was a grin. She was playing with him and his emotions went from concern, to anger, to passion. "I ought to pick you up and take you to my bed and make love to you for the rest of the afternoon."

"I dare you," is all she said.

"You are just a little tease," he said.

"You'll never know until you try."

Pete got up, walked around the desk and took Alice's hand and said, "I can't carry you but by damn, I can sure lead you. Let's go to bed."

"Somehow I don't know if you really want too. You might be sorry later," she continued teasing, and it was making him want her all the more.

As they passed through his bedroom door, Alice had already come out of her blouse and he begun to reach for the hooks on her brassiere when the door bell rang. "Damn," mumbled Pete. "I have to answer that." He pulled his bedroom door closed and started toward the front door.

Opening the front door, Pete saw it was the woman who was cleaning his apartment. He had forgotten that today was her day to clean. She would be here for at least three hours. "Come on in and you can start in Alice's office." Pete hoped by the time she finished her office, he would be back at his desk.

When Pete went back into his bedroom, he found Alice without her blouse or bra, lying on the bed. "I wanted to be ready in case you could get rid of them."

Pete wasn't in a good mood at all, he said, "Well, I couldn't. It's the cleaning woman. She'll be here for three hours. You better get dressed."

"The mood you're in, I might as well stay dressed," replied Alice as she put her bra and blouse back on. "I guess it wasn't meant to be."

+++++

It was 4:10 p.m. when Sanders set the plane down in Atlanta. He had called ahead and rented a car at National Car Rental. While he was picking out a mid-sized car, he picked up a map of the city. He also made sure the car had a GPS available. Before leaving the lot, he plugged in the address, 6758 Cogbill Road, Atlanta. The GPS told him he was twenty four miles away and it should take him twenty nine minutes to get there.

During the drive, Sanders called Gracie to let her know he had landed the plane and was on his way to Carol's resident. Gracie said, "I have a couple of stops to make before I relieve Sue at the hospital. If anything has changed with Carol I'll call you. You be sure and call me before you start home. Love you more."

Then he called Pete to see if anything new was going on. Pete sounded like he was in a bad mood, but Sanders couldn't figure out why.

At the house on Cogbill Road, Sanders could see a 2011 silver Lexus in the drive. He couldn't remember the license number of the Lexus Carol was driving during the first attempt on Pete's life, but this one sure fit the description. The house was in an upscale neighborhood. It was a red brick with about 3500 square feet. On the side of the house he could see a large fireplace.

Sanders parked his car beside the Lexus, walked to the front door and rang the bell. No answer. Then he rang it again. On the third attempt, a man who looked to be around thirty five opened the door. His hair was wet and not combed. He was wearing a robe and looked as though he had just gotten out of the shower. "My name is Sanders and I work for the Dover Detective Agency in Memphis. I would like to talk with you about Carol Wooten."

"Carol's out of town, I'm not sure when she will be back."

"I know that. She is in the hospital in Memphis and she has been critical for a couple of days, replied Sanders.

The young man inside the house seemed surprised and must have believed Sanders because he invited him in and asked him to sit down. "My name is Rick Rice. Carol and I have been together for about four years. What do you mean, she is in the hospital?"

"How much do you know about Carol?"

"I know we have a good life together. Her job requires her to be out of town a lot, but it also gives her a lot of time off."

"Do you know what she does when she is out of town?"

"She is a sales rep for several products. Did you say she is critical?"

He didn't know why, but Sanders believed Rice was telling the truth. He said, "Rice, you had better sat down, I have a story to tell you and then I would hope you have some information for me."

Rice couldn't believe Carol was a "hit man", although he knew she loved to fire her weapons. Together, they had spent a lot of time on the firing range. "I thought it was just something she enjoyed doing. I had no idea she was perfecting her job!"

"What I need is the name of the person who hired her. Do you have any idea who it could have been?"

"No, but I do know that she has two cell phones. I would tease her about that, but she would always say, 'One is for business and one is for pleasure. She never gave me the number of her business phone."

"Well, thank you for your time. You know what I need. If you run across anything that might help, call me. Carol is in ICU at Baptist East in Memphis." Sanders gave Rice his card as he left.

After Sanders had left, Rice went to the phone and called a person who he only knew as "Chief".

Chapter Eighteen

Helena
Deliveries
June 25-28

Ruby had gone to Big Island with Mike for a dance. The two of them had been getting along great. There was just one problem that she didn't know how to handle. Frank, one of the three powerbrokers, continued to "come-on" to her. She knew he knew more about the drug ring than Mike. It could be that she could get more information for Operation Delta Pride from Frank than she could from Mike. Then again, Frank could be setting her up, showing Mike how fickle she was. She had to be careful.

Ruby had decided Frank was really just a dirty old man who enjoyed touching but couldn't "get it up" if he had to. Therefore, it would do no harm to continue to give back as good as she got. The important thing was to continue to "play-up" to Mike. She knew he was going to Little Rock on June 26th and Fayetteville on the 27th and 28th. She already had been invited to Fayetteville; somehow she needed to wrangle an invitation for Little Rock, as well.

She wasn't sure how it had happened, but by the time Mike left her apartment he had promised to pick her up

Tuesday at 8:00 a.m. for the trip to Little Rock. She would need to remember to take her small camera. It was small enough to carry in her purse and maybe she would be able to take some pictures for evidence.

+++++

Sanders landed his plane back in Memphis at 11:00 p.m. and immediately went to the hospital to see Gracie. Sanders wanted to know about Carol's condition and about the attempt made on her life. Gracie told him her condition was about the same. She was awake more but still not saying anything that made sense.

Gracie wanted to know about the trip Sanders had made to Atlanta. He told her he had met the boyfriend, Rick Rice. Sanders said, "Personally, I was impressed with Rice and believed him when he said he knew nothing of Carol working as a hit man. However, I have not checked him out in any way. He did tell me he would be coming to Memphis as soon as he could clear it with his boss."

+++++

Ruby had been up for a while. She didn't know why, but she was nervous about the trip to Little Rock. At 7:30, she was dressed and waiting for Mike to come by and pick her up. With thirty minutes to kill, she called Pete to check in with him. Alice had answered the phone and told her Pete was cooking breakfast for them this morning, but that she would relieve him so he could talk on the phone.

Alice had been very businesslike since the interruption by the cleaning woman. Nothing had been said about their personal issues. Alice had hoped that Pete was up early and cooking breakfast as an apology for the things he had said and done the night before.

"Pete, you're wanted on the phone. It's Ruby. You want me to relieve you at the stove?"

"Yeah." Alice couldn't tell by his short answer what kind of mood he was in, but she had the feeling he was still pissed. As she handed him the phone and took over the job of preparing breakfast, she thought, "Maybe, I need to get my boss to get someone else to come in and protect Pete? He sure doesn't look happy."

Ruby told Pete that she was going to Little Rock with Mike. Mike had told her that he had a meeting which would last an hour and would drop her off at the mall. She suspected that he was making a delivery. "Mike should be here in about thirty minutes."

"Ruby, you told me all this last night. Why are you really calling me?

"Boy, aren't you in a good mood this morning."

"I'm sorry for the way I said it, but you had already told me about your trip with Mike and I can't help but feel like there is another reason for your call."

"I'm nervous about something and can't figure out what," responded Ruby.

"Something about the trip?" asked Pete.

"I guess so. I'm convinced he's making a delivery and I need to know where he's taking the stuff and who he's taking it to."

Pete took his time answering her. "I'm just thinking out loud, but what if I send someone to follow Mike after he lets you out."

"That might work, but how are you going to know where he plans to let me out?"

"You could tell him you need to go to the Dillard's in North Little Rock and we could have an FBI Agent waiting for you. Would that make you feel better?"

"Yes, I think it would. Plan on us being there about 10:00 a.m. and Pete, thanks."

As soon as Pete hung up the phone, he went to his desk and looked up a number. As he was dialing it, Alice said, "Your breakfast is getting cold."

"I'm calling Agent Soden in Little Rock. The family worked with him in finding my cousin, Susan."

Soden answered his phone with, "This is FBI Agent Soden, what can I do for you?"

"Officer Soden, I'm an attorney working for the Department of Justice in Memphis. My name is Pete Dover and I believe you worked with the Dover Detective Agency, and former FBI Agent Jerry Sanders a couple of years ago with a kidnapping case which involved Susan Eason."

"You got me. How is Sanders and what can I do for you?"

Pete caught Soden up on the family. Then, he told him about the big drug case, Operation Delta Pride, which he was working on. "I have an undercover agent who will be dropped off at Dillard's in North Little Rock while a drug delivery is being made. What I need is for you to follow the delivery pickup and gather evidence. We need to know when and where the delivery was made and if possible, the people involved in receiving the drugs."

Soden and Pete continued to talk about the details and Soden said, "I think I can handle that. I'll get back to you as soon as the driver, who made the delivery, picks up your agent at Dillard's."

During the time Pete was on the phone, Alice had put bacon, eggs, biscuits and gravy on the table. By the time Pete hung up, Alice was through eating. As she got up and started toward her bedroom, she said with an attitude, "Your eggs are cold."

The air in the apartment was thick enough to cut with a knife. Pete was being forced to either make love to her or ask her to leave. There could be no in-between. Pete knew something had to change and quick.

+++++

By 10:00 a.m. Ruby was in the mall in North Little Rock. She had convinced Mike that only Dillards had the shoes she wanted. She had seen them in a Dillard's catalog and when she called she was told that was the only store that had that particular shoe. At least that's what she had told Mike and he had believed her. Now she had to find a new pair of shoes to show him when he returned.

Meanwhile, Soden had watched as Ruby got out of Mike's pickup. When the pickup left the parking lot, Soden was following. He followed Mike to a warehouse at 2369 East Hwy 70 in North Little Rock. The overhead door was raised as Mike turned into the warehouse; however, it took a while for the door to close. This meant that Soden had time to park his car and slip through the door before it closed.

The warehouse was filled with tires of all sizes and shapes and in the very back was a tire changing machine. That was where the red pickup was parked and two men had begun to work on the tires. They broke down the tires, took out the pot and remounted the tires. Then, they lowered the spare and took more pot out from somewhere under the truck bed. Mike was given a briefcase to check out. After he looked in it, it was place somewhere under the truck bed and the spare was raised to its normal position. The whole exchange took less than thirty minutes.

Soden had been using his Canon PowerShot to record a video for the entire scene. He was especially careful to get some good still pictures of the person who handed Mike the briefcase filled with money. Then he hurried back to the overhead door to wait for it to open so he could slip out and follow Mike back to the mall where he was to pick up Ruby.

+++++

Just as Pete opened the door to Alice's bedroom, he saw her stepping out of the shower. She hadn't seen him. He watched her as she used the towel to dry herself. When she had finished she dried her hair again and wrapped the towel around her head. With only the towel around her head, she started into the bedroom. "What do you want?" Alice asked when she saw him watching her.

"You," he said with hoarseness in his voice.

"You have had a terrible way of showing it. For days I've been rubbing it all over you and all you did was push me away."

Pete walked toward her, looked deep into her eyes and said, "I didn't mean to. I didn't want to and I won't today" Then he took the towel off her head, put his arms around her nude body and kissed her deeply.

+++++

Rick Rice bumped into Andy, Sanders and Sue coming out of the hospital cafeteria as he was entering the hospital. Sanders recognized him and called to him. "Rice, wait a minute, I want to introduce you to some of my family. This is Andy and Sue Dover. Andy is my wife's brother and my boss."

"Good to meet you," he said. "Where is ICU. I haven't seen Carol and I'm kind of anxious to see how she is doing."

Sue said, "I don't blame you. I'm going to ICU now and I would be glad to show you the way. You know hospitals. You can get lost in them."

There wasn't much said as Sue and Rice walked to the elevator and on to ICU. However, Sue was not sure about Rice. She wasn't sure what it was, but something just didn't feel right as she took him into ICU to see Carol.

Carol was conscious when Rice and Sue went in to see her. When Carol saw Rice there was something in her eyes that told Sue she was afraid of him. The words she tried to say didn't seem to make sense. However, in spite of all that, Rice did speak words of love and comfort to Carol.

A nurse came into the room and told Rice and Sue that visiting hours were over and they would have to leave. They could come back in three hours; at 4:00 p.m. Sue stood at the door and waited for Rice to tell Carol that he would be back.

Once they were back in the ICU waiting room, Rice told Sue he was going to leave the hospital for a while and that he would try to be back in time for the next visitation time with Carol. Sue said, "I'm going to be here until 6:00 p.m. and then Gracie, Sanders' wife, will come and sit with her until 6:00 in the morning."

+++++

Detectives Searcy and Melton, who had made an appointment to see Sanders at his office, introduced themselves to the secretary, who was filling in for Sue. She took them back to Sanders' office and he invited them to come in and take a load off. "Good to see you two, hope you got some good news about the bad guys," said Sanders.

"I really wish we did, but the truth is we seem to be going over the same ground and getting nowhere. I thought maybe you could help us move forward if we just talked about the whole case together," responded Melton.

Together, the three men reviewed key elements of the case. They concluded this case is different because the hit-man is in custody but the person who hired her is unknown. Often it's the other way around. The detectives revealed the results they had found on the cell phones. One of the phones had a lot of calls. Most of those calls were made to a man named Rick Rice.

"I can help you with Rice. I went to Atlanta to see where Carol lived. There I found a boyfriend of four years, named Rick Rice. My first impression was that he was one of the good guys and knew nothing of Carol's job as a hit-man. He is in Memphis now. I just saw him at the hospital. What about the second phone?"

Searcy said, "There were very few calls made or received on this phone. Every call was to or from a 'private number'. So far we have not been able to learn who was making those calls, but we believe the 'private number' calls were from the person who hired her."

Sanders was careful not to reveal anything about Operation Delta Pride. He hated for them to be working partially in the dark, but Pete had made him swear not to talk about it.

+++++

Pete sat behind his desk with Ruby, Sanders and Alice in front of him. As he looked at them he wondered, "What the hell is going on?" After the trip to Little Rock, Ruby had called and asked for an appointment to see him. Soden had already emailed his report. Therefore, he set up this meeting and called Sanders and asked him to join them.

He also asked Alice to sit in on the meeting. At least in regard to Alice, he knew what was going on and really felt good about it. What he didn't know about was Ruby and Sanders. He saw Sanders' face light up when he saw Ruby and he watched a sudden mood change take place with Ruby.

Finally, Sanders said, "Pete, we owe you an explanation. You see, Ruby and I knew each other in another life. We worked together in New Orleans as FBI agents. She was just beginning and I was coming to the end."

"I didn't realize I had never told you the name of our undercover agent in Helena and I had no idea you would know her." As Alice watched the body language of Sanders and Ruby she was sure they had know each other in the "biblical sense" but that wasn't any of her business.

With the personal stuff out of the way, the group went on to talk about the trip to Little Rock. Things seemed to have gone well. With Soden's help they had gathered some valuable evidence and, of course, Ruby had gained a new pair of shoes.

Moving on to the trip to Fayetteville, Ruby told them it sounded like the same kind of delivery. "We are to drive to Fayetteville tomorrow and the meeting is Thursday morning at 8:00. He plans for me to sleep in during the meeting. I am sure what Mike calls a meeting will actually be a delivery."

"Could we run the same kinds of operation that we did in Little Rock?" asked Pete. "The only problem is, I don't know an FBI agent in Fayetteville."

"I don't either," said Ruby.

"What if I flew the jet to Fayetteville, rented a car and followed Mike from the motel when he left for his meeting?" asked Sanders.

"That might work if Gracie will let you," said Alice half serious and half joking.

With everything set for the delivery, Sanders handed Ruby his phone number and asked her to call as soon as she could after she found out the motel where they would be staying.

Pete wanted to ask for advice. "All of you have a lot of time invested in this operation; therefore, I want to give you a chance to voice your opinion. Debra Witcher, my boss, is beginning to put pressure on me to wrap up this operation. What do you think I ought to do?"

"Do you have enough to convict?" asked Sanders.

"As I look at 'the plan" that was written by Janie, I believe we have enough to convict the little people and maybe most of the middle people, but we really don't have any idea who the 'chief' is. Since Janie was involved, it was probably someone with Sneed, Weeks and King, but we don't know who."

Ruby said, "I've put too much of myself into this not to complete the job. If you're asking for my vote---I vote to continue."

"If Ruby wants to continue, I vote with her," said Sanders.

"Okay then, Sanders, can you get the family working hard to solve the rest of our puzzle here in Memphis? Ruby, I'm convinced that Joe Cole is the connection between Helena and Memphis. See what you can find out. In the meantime, I'll put Debra off as long as I can."

+++++

As Sanders walked into Andy's office he was thinking about what he wanted to say to Andy. Soon after he had left Pete's, he called Andy to ask if he was going to be at the office for a while. He wanted to update Andy as to the direction of the investigation. The family, without much luck, had been trying to find out who tried to kill Pete. Pete, now, wanted them to focus on the question, "Who is the 'chief' of the drug ring?" It might be the same person, but the focus of the investigation would be different.

After the small talk, Sanders said, "I've just come from Pete's and a meeting with the undercover FBI agent in Helena. Pete feels we have enough evidence to convict most of the little people and some of the middle people in Operation Delta Pride. He wants us to focus on finding the 'chief' or leader. Pete believes this person is in Memphis."

"What does this mean? What does he want us to do?"

"Go back to the beginning of our investigation. Focus on Charles Schuler and Robert Shelby and their attorneys who are a part of the Sneed, Weeks and King firm. Pete believes somewhere in that mix, we will find our man."

"Sanders, what do you think?"

"We may well find our man somewhere in the law firm, but I also wonder if we ought to check out the US Attorney's Office. I don't understand why Debra Witcher is putting pressure on Pete to close the case without finding the chief. I also understand that when Pete was shot and she removed Charles Schuler and Robert Shelby from his case load, she never reassigned Robert Shelby to another attorney."

Andy and Sanders continued to discuss the case. Sanders told Andy that he was taking the jet to Fayetteville to back up Ruby. "We really don't have any evidence as to the Fayetteville people involved in this case. I will leave here about noon tomorrow."

"Just be careful. You're running blind on this one. By the way, tell me about Rick Rice."

Sanders told Andy he didn't know a lot. That he had met him in Atlanta when he went to check out Carol. "He said he and Carol had been together for four years and that he thought she worked as a sales rep for several products. At the time, I thought he was being honest with me, however, after talking with Sue, I'm not so sure."

"That's what I wanted to know; because Sue is convinced something is not right. Sue was at the hospital all day yesterday and didn't see Rice. She wondered what kind of boyfriend he was if he had only been to the hospital once to check on her, especially after driving all the way from Atlanta."

"If Sam has the time, maybe you need to ask him to keep an eye on Rice," replied Sanders. "Right now I'm going home to try to spend some quality time with Gracie. With her working nights and me working days, I've missed her."

+++++

As Sanders waited for Mike to leave the Holiday Inn, he remembered his experiences with Ruby when they were working in New Orleans. She had been a good partner on and off the job. It was a lifetime ago, but he couldn't help remembering the nights they had made love until dawn and then slept until noon. He also remembered that last night when they had solved Susan's kidnapping case. At that time he had told Ruby he had decided to ask Gracie to marry him, but that fact hadn't stopped Ruby. After the celebration dinner, she offered to "go to bed with him" one last time before he married Gracie. Sanders had told her "no" and had never regretted it.

Around 4:30 yesterday afternoon, Ruby had called and given Sanders the name of their motel and that Mike's meeting was 8:00 a.m. It was now 7:30 a.m. and Mike was coming out of their motel to get in his pickup. Sanders was glad the pickup was red. It made it easier to follow.

Twenty-five minutes later, Mike pulled his pickup into a tire warehouse. The overhead door closed immediately. Sanders never had a chance to park and follow Mike on foot. He would have to find another way to gather the evidence. He remembered that Soden had said the tire changing machine in Little Rock was in the back of the warehouse. Sanders parked and began to walk around the outside of the building.

About seventy-five feet from the street, two cars were parked. One was a new black BMW and the other was an older model Chevy. Sanders carefully approached the cars to find them both empty. Then, he saw a door behind the BMW and figured that the passengers of the cars entered the warehouse through that door. He was glad he had his tool kit to open the door if he needed too; however, he found the door was unlocked.

Very quietly and slowly Sanders opened the door. Large tires were stacked about ten foot all around him. Looking down a walking pathway, he could see light about thirty-feet away from him. The pathway was barely large enough for him to walk through. As he approached the light he could see it was an opening and he could hear people talking.

He got his camera ready and slowly walked until he could see Mike and the people around his pickup. Stepping back into the dark a bit, he began to take pictures of two men who were taking what appeared to be drugs out of the tires. Then a man who was well dressed brought out a briefcase and handed it to Mike. Mike opened the briefcase and took out three stacks of money as he seemed to count it. When he was satisfied, he put the briefcase in a box and placed it under the bed of the pickup.

Sanders decided he had enough evidence and he didn't want to get locked in the warehouse, so he slipped out the way he had entered the warehouse. When the delivery was complete, Mike drove his pickup out of the warehouse while the other three men came out the side door and got in their cars. Just to be sure he didn't miss anything; Sanders followed Mike back to the Holiday Inn.

Chapter Nineteen

Memphis
New Focus
June 29

    At the staff meeting of the Dover Detective Agency on Friday, Andy and Sanders talked about the change of focus the investigation was taking. Sue was concerned that not enough attention was going to be given to find the person who had shot Pete. Sanders told her he believed if we find the "chief" in the Operation Delta Pride investigation then we would have the person who hired someone to kill Pete. Other members of the agency agreed with Sanders and together they finally got Sue on board with the new focus.

    Sam had completed his work on the McClintock case, so he was ready for a new challenge. Andy gave him an overview of Rick Rice and asked him to keep an eye on him. Sue told the group that she had only seen Rice twice in the five days he had been in Memphis. She said, "I have watched Carol's eyes when he is in the room and I see something that I can only describe as fear. I tell you there is something wrong in that relationship. By the way, Carol seems to be getting stronger but is still not able to communicate."

Finishing up the meeting, Andy said, "I want Sanders to work with Pete and also check out what is happening with Charles Schuler and Robert Shelby. I will try to find a link to someone at the Sneed, Weeks and King's law firm. If anyone has any extra time, call me. I would like to have someone poke around Debra Witcher's office. Oh, I almost forgot Gracie will you talk with Al and Sally and catch them up on our new focus and tell them we will be in touch?"

+++++

The chief had instructed Rice to keep him up to date on Carol's condition. So, when his private phone rang he was not surprised when it was Rice who was calling. "I just finished talking with Carol's doctor and he tells me that she may well pull through. He is concerned about her lack of ability to communicate but feels that in time she will regain that ability."

"You must stay close by and if it appears that she could regain that ability, you have to take her out."

Rice responds, "When I'm in her room and look at her, it's as though she knows why I'm here. All I see is fear."

"She's a smart girl. If her mind is right, she knows. Keep in touch and do your job."

+++++

It had been four days since Pete and Alice had first made love. Pete was not sure he would ever understand women. Their relationship was still a kind of love/hate relationship. When things were good, they were very good. But when it was bad, it was very bad. Thankfully, today was one of the good days. It began with Alice slipping into Pete's bed and waking him by planting wet kisses all over his body. And of course, Pete responded as any American male would.

They showered, had a good breakfast and were late getting to their desk. At 10:00 a.m. the phone rang. It was

Ruby. "I haven't talked with Sanders. Was he able to get the evidence?"

"Yes, in fact I have the pictures in front of me. They show the exchange and give us a good picture of the people involved. I'm having the FBI do a background of each of them so we will be ready to go when the time is right. You did good. How was the trip for you?"

"I feel guilty. I was supposed to be working but I really enjoyed myself. Mike is an excellent lover. It's just too bad he is one of the bad guys. The other reason I called is to let you know there is another big dance at Big Island Saturday night and Mike has asked me to go. Joe Cole is usually at those dances. I will try to get close to him."

"Just be careful, HE is definitely one of the bad guys."

+++++

Sanders had made an appointment with Debra Witcher. Since he had spent much of his life with the FBI he felt he was the one to really ask her the hard questions. He had never worked with her and sitting across the desk from her caused him to feel that he didn't know her at all. However, he knew the system and he knew a US Attorney in charge didn't like to be questioned. Sanders wasn't sure how much Pete had told her about his involvement in Operation Delta Pride, so he planned to stay away from that subject, if he could.

"What can I do for you today?" asked Witcher.

"We haven't had much luck finding the person who killed Janie and tried to kill Pete, so we are regrouping and retracing some of our work."

"How does that involve me? I was under the impression that it was Carol Wooten who killed Janie and tried to kill Pete"

"Yes, we know it was Carol who pulled the trigger but we don't know who hired her. However, we have reason to believe that it could have been either Charles Schuler or Robert Shelby. Since Pete was the pretrial attorney of record, I'm here to find out what has happened to their cases. Who is the attorney that is to take them to trial?"

As expected, Witcher got very defensive. "I assigned the cases to Erma Moore but I don't understand what that has got to do with anything."

"Has a new trial date been set?"

"As I said, I don't understand what that has to do with anything you're investigating?"

Sanders had been in the business long enough that he was not going to let Witcher intimidate him. He said, "If one of these two men hired the hit man, then it has everything to do with our investigation. You can sandbag me if you want to, but we will get the information we need to do our job."

Realizing that Sanders had been around the block at time or two, Witcher said, "I'm sorry if you thought I was sandbagging you. I'm the kind of person who likes to keep the Department of Justice business within the Department of Justice. How can I help you?"

"As I said, I'm here to discover who was assigned to the cases of Charles Schuler and Robert Shelby. I also need to know when their trials come up,"

"I've already told you the cases were assigned to Erma Moore. I can't give you more information than that."

"Ms Witcher, let me be blunt. The word is out that Robert Shelby's case has been dismissed and I'm here to find out why."

Standing up, Witcher said, "Mr. Sanders, your appointment with me is over. I'm telling you to leave."

Sanders stood up, walked toward the door, turned to face Witcher and said, "Ms. Witcher, I will find the information that I need to do my job and I truly hope that it does not lead me back to you."

Getting in his car, Sanders called Pete and said, "You may get a call from Debra Witcher. I just left her office and I didn't leave her a happy camper. I hope I didn't do you any damage."

+++++

Rice intentionally waited until the last visiting time of the day to visit Carol. It was 8:00 p.m. and many of the doctors, nurses and visitors had already left the hospital leaving only a few people around. Sue had told Gracie that Carol had been resting peacefully all day. Gracie was in Carol's room holding her hand, talking to her and trying to make sense of her words when Rice entered Carol's room.

"I'm Rick Rice," he said to Gracie.

"I'm Gracie Sanders, you met my husband in Atlanta."

"Yes, I remember him. It's good to meet you," Rice said as he walked up to Carol's bed.

As Gracie moved aside, she continued to watch Carol and she saw that look, which Sue had described as fear, in Carol's face. Carol had also quit trying to talk. Rice took her hand and spoke words of comfort to her; however, Carol was becoming very agitated.

Looking at Gracie, Rice asked, "Could we be alone for a few minutes?"

Gracie was looking at Carol when Rice had asked and saw her look to Gracie and say, "Stay." It was the first word she had understood, but there was no doubt, she asked Gracie to stay in the room with her while Rice was there. Gracie was not sure if Rice heard her.

Gracie responded to Rice with, "I'm sorry, I can't leave the room. The police have asked us to have someone present with her at all times. The police guard takes a break when I'm here, so I have to stay." Gracie noticed Carol seemed to relax some as Gracie spoke to Rice.

Rice wanted to argue but knew it would do no good. Besides it would bring suspicious on him when Carol died. So he told Carol he loved her and left the room. Gracie resumed her place beside Carol and listened as she tried to speak. Gracie thought she could make out the word, "thanks" from Carol.

It was becoming clear to Gracie that Carol's mind was alright. It was the ability to communicate that was the problem and that was getting better.

+++++

Rice really didn't want to call the chief but he knew he had better give him the word as soon as he could, so as soon as he got in his car he called and said, "I did the best I could but the Sanders woman wouldn't leave me alone with Carol, so I couldn't get my job done."

"I'm sorry to hear that. That means I'll have to get someone else to take care of it," the chief said.

Rice knew what "I'm sorry to hear that" meant. It meant there would be no more jobs coming from the chief and it could even mean his life was in danger. "Please, give me one more chance to get it done."

"It has to be done by this time tomorrow, she is a real danger to all of us," the chief said as he hung up the phone.

What Rice did not know was that he was being followed. Sam had caught up with him in the hospital and was now following him as they left the parking lot.

+++++

Andy was in the Sneed, Weeks and King's law firm building. He had made an appointment with Bob Wilkins, who had been Janie's boss, and was waiting. After some time, the secretary said, "Mr. Dover, Mr. Wilkins will see you now. Please follow me."

As Andy walked into Wilkins' office, Wilkins stood and said, "Mr. Dover, it is so good to see you. Please have a seat and let's see how I can help you."

After shaking hands both men sat down and Wilkins began by saying, "I believe I had an appointment with your father some time back. I'm sorry I had to cancel. I never knew what he wanted to discuss."

"Dad wanted to talk with you about Janie Albert. I believe she worked for you."

"Actually, Janie worked for Sneed, Weeks and King; however, at the time she was killed she had been doing research for me. I have truly missed her. She was very capable with anything we asked her to do."

Andy asked, "Do you have any idea why she was killed?"

"I assumed the shooter was trying to kill Pete Dover and Janie was in the wrong place at the wrong time."

"That may be true, but we have reason to believe that it could have been the opposite of that. Maybe Pete was in the wrong place," responded Andy.

"What makes you think that," asked Wilkins.

Andy wasn't about to tell Wilkins about "the plan" that had been found in some of Janie's papers, but he did tell Wilkins that Janie was the one that had called Pete and had wanted to meet with him.

"I figured that would be because she was sweet on Pete and wanted to rekindle their relationship."

"That could be true, but we don't think so."

Andy and Wilkins continued to spar back and forth. Neither was able to get the advantage, although Andy was sure that Wilkins knew more than he was saying. Then Andy said, "I want to change the subject. Not only did I come here to ask about Janie I also have heard that you are the lead attorney for Charles Schuler and Robert Shelby."

"That's true, although the case against Robert Shelby has been dropped by the Department of Justice."

"Can you tell me why it was dropped?" asked Andy.

"I don't know if I would tell you if I knew, however I simply don't know. I believe there wasn't enough evidence to convict. After Pete was shot and a new attorney was assigned, the case was dropped, which is not that unusual."

"What about the case against Charles Schuler?"

"That case is set for July 28th, and I will represent Mr. Schuler," responded Wilkins.

"Anything you can tell me about that case?"

"Not really. It will be a hard case for us to win. I believe Erma Moore will be the Department of Justice lead attorney. She is a very good lawyer."

"Was Erma Moore the person who made the decision to drop the Shelby case?"

"I wasn't privy to that information," responded Wilkins.

Let me ask you one last question, "Do you know an attorney from Helena named Joe Cole?"

"Joe and I went to law school together. Why do you ask?"

"His name comes up from time to time. I was just trying to get some background on him."

"Joe's a good guy. We've had some good times together."

+++++

Sanders stopped by Pete's in order to pick Pete's brain about Charles Schuler and Robert Shelby. All he really knew was that Schuler was a bad guy charged with murder and that Shelby was a supposedly good guy charged with money laundering. He wanted to know everything possible before he interviewed the two people. However, his visit with Pete begins with a discussion about Pete's boss, Debra Witcher.

Pete said, "You might ought to watch yourself around Witcher. After your meeting, she called me. Let me just say it this way, she don't like you none."

"I'm not sure how I feel about her. I wanted to put her on notice that we are willing to go anywhere, say whatever we need to and do whatever is necessary to uncover who's responsible for killing Janie and tried to kill you. I'm sorry if I hurt her feeling by suggesting she could be a suspect. I hope she doesn't hold it against you."

Sanders wasn't really worried about Witcher. He wanted to move on so he said, "Tell me what you can about Schuler and Shelby. I need to know all I can before I interview them."

"You're going to see Schuler and Shelby?"

"Thought I would; what can you tell me about them?"

Pete began a long story of Schuler's problems. "He is a typical crime boss. He has several people working for him. Johnny is in charge of the girls and made sure each of them earned their money by the hour while lying on their back. Don takes care of his drug trafficking. Mickey is the loan shark person.

One night Schuler went with Mickey to collect a large loan and they got too rough. The man died and there were witnesses. That's the night the police charged Schuler and Mickey with murder. When you go see him, watch your back."

Sanders assured Pete he didn't intend to get himself killed. "Gracie wouldn't like it. Now, what do you know about Shelby?"

Pete begins another long story about how Shelby seems like a good productive church-going citizen. He is a family man with a wife and two children. He never lets you see anything to complain about. However, he is using his supermarkets for money laundering. The FBI has built a solid case.

"Pete, do you know how he's doing it?"

"It's a complex plan, but basically the first step is called 'placement'. This step is when dirty money is inserted into a legitimate financial institution. Shelby is doing this in the form of bank deposits from his supermarkets. If the deposits are kept below $10,000 each, the bank does not have to report the transactions. This is the riskiest step. Most of our evidence against Shelby takes place in this step.

The second step is called 'layering'. This is just sending the money through various financial transactions to change its form and make it hard to follow. This is the most complex step in their laundering scheme, and it is all about making the original dirty money as hard to trace as possible.

Finally, there is what is called 'integration', which is when the money re-enters the main economy in legitimate-looking form – it appears to come from a legal transaction. At this point, Shelby and his associates can use the money without getting caught. It is almost impossible to catch a launderer during the 'integration' step if there is no documentation during the previous stages."

"If you have the evidence, why would Witcher drop the case?"

"I've been thinking about that for some time. I'm convinced it's totally political. Someone out there has put pressure on her to drop it," answered Pete.

+++++

Rice had been working for the man he only knew as "Chief" for several years. In fact, the chief had been the one who got him into this middleman role. For several years now he had been the one the chief called when he needed someone killed. Once in a while he would do the job himself, but most of the time he would contract with someone else. That's how he got the nickname, "contractor".

Rice had met Carol in a bar in Atlanta. One thing led to another and they moved in together. It was some time before he learned she was an excellent marksman who loved to spend time on the firing range. One day she overheard him talking to the chief on the phone and after he had hung up she surprised him and said, "I'd like to take that job." And she talked him into giving her the job. He remembered how nervous he was and how he had guided her through the process. She actually did the job well and fell in love with the work. The job with Janie and Pete was her first miss in eleven jobs. It was too bad how that was working out.

Now, Carol had to be taken out, and because of the Dover women, he couldn't do it. He had to find a doctor or nurse to do it and he had to do it quick. Luckily, he had seen a nurse who was with Carol that he had known before. As he remembered her she was the type person who would do anything for enough money. She would be perfect for the job because everyone knew her as a nurse involved in Carol's case.

Looking at his watch he wondered if it was too late to call her. It was 10:30 p.m. he decided to take a chance and dialed her number.

"Hey, this is Anita," he heard as he put the phone to his ear.

"Anita, this is Rick Rice. I hope I'm not calling too late."

"No, you're not. I'm just now getting off from work. Gosh, it has been a long time since I've heard from you. How have you been?"

"I've been good. I'm in Memphis and since you just got off from work I'm wondering if we might meet and have a late dinner."

"I'm starved. Where should we meet?"

"This is your town. You make that decision."

"There is a good place called 'Bobs' that is not far from the hospital. It stays open all night. I could meet you."

"Sounds good. I'm looking forward to seeing you in thirty minutes."

Sam began to follow as Rice came out of his motel room, got in his car and pulled out of the parking lot. Sam had an idea that something was happening. He couldn't figure out why a man with his girlfriend in the hospital would be leaving his motel room unless something was happening with Carol. So he called Gracie who was on duty at the hospital and asked if anything had changed. She told him everything seemed to be normal.

Sam continued to follow and watched as Rice pulled up in front of Bob's. Rice went into the restaurant and sat down at a table with a very attractive woman, who seemed glad to see him. Looking through the window, Sam could see she had long brown hair and when she stood up to hug Rice, he could see she was tall sporty looking person who was wearing a nurse's uniform.

On the inside of the restaurant the conversation began with catch-up small talk, as Rice and Anita remembered their past together and shared what had been happening in their lives recently. Before they had finished their dinner, Anita asked Rice to spend the night at her house instead of that cold motel room and Rice had quickly agreed.

Chapter Twenty

Memphis
Murder
June 30

When Sam had followed Rice to Anita's apartment, he knew it was going to be a long night. He called his wife, Daisy, and told her where he was and what he was doing. Then he settled in for a long night. Sam found the apartment manager's phone number and was able to find out from him, the woman in apartment 17 was Anita Knox. He just couldn't figure out the whole situation. Rice had been with Carol for four years and while she was critical in the hospital he was shacking up with, what appeared to be, an old flame.

The night had been an exciting one for Rice, as he and Anita remembered why they had enjoyed being with each other in the past. At breakfast, which Anita had cooked, Rice decided it was time to get down to business. Anita was not surprised to find out that Rice was involved with some shady people or even that he had killed people for money. However, she was shocked out of her mind when he asked her to kill Carol.

"Why would I do that?" she asked.
"For $100,000," he said.

When Anita responded with, "Now, that's a reason I could live with," Rice knew he had her. It might take some time to work out the details, but he knew in the end she would do the job.

+++++

Anita had clocked in at 10:00 a.m. and to tell the truth she was not focused on her work. All she could think about was what she was about to do for $100,000. She had done some unethical things for money before, but nothing like this and never for this kind of money. "What would she do with $100,000?" she thought. "Don't spend it before you get it," she heard her mom say to her as she had hundreds of times before she died. Anita considered the noon hour the best time. Several of the staff would be taking a lunch break and visiting hour didn't come until 2:00. Almost no one would be around. She would be alone.

When the policeman who was guarding the door went for a cup of coffee and Sue was in the bathroom, Anita knew the time had come. Anita was in Carol's room alone. Thanks goodness Carol was sleeping. She didn't know if she could do it with her looking at her. Anita took a pillow from one of the chairs, placed it over Carol's face and held it. When the machines started making their beeping sound, Anita knew it was over.

Quickly, she put the pillow back in the chair and left the room. There was confusion as several nurses, including Anita, appeared to go into Carol's room. A crash cart was called, and they worked for thirty minutes. However, she was gone. The job was done. Now, all Anita had to do was call Rice and collect her money.

The ICU doctor went into the waiting room to tell Sue. He said, "I thought she was on the road to recovery, but apparently she had too much damage. Heart quit beating and we couldn't bring her back. I'm sorry. I know you wanted her to tell you who hired her to kill your son. Do you know who we need to notify?"

"Rick Rice is the only one I know. He's her boyfriend and has been here a couple of times. I know he is from Atlanta but I don't have his phone number."

As soon as the doctor left, Sue called Andy and told him what had happened. Andy knew there had been an attempt on Carol's life before and asked Sue if thought someone had killed her or if she had died as a result of Alice's gunshot.

"Andy, I don't really know. The doctor seemed to think that her heart simply gave out, but I don't know. I had just stepped into the bathroom when it happened."

+++++

When Anita called Rice to let him know it was over, they made a date to meet at her apartment at 10:30 p.m. for the pay-off and maybe another night together. Then, Rice called the chief and told him that Carol was dead.

"That's good," said the chief. "I'll get back to you about Pete Dover later. Nothing has to be done immediately."

Rice had received a call while he was talking to the chief and now he noticed they had left him a voicemail which told him that Carol had died and he needed to come to the hospital immediately.

+++++

Posing as a news reporter, Sanders had been waiting for his appointment with Robert Shelby. As he waited, his mind was on the conversation he had with Pete. This whole "money laundering" issue was interesting to Sanders. He couldn't help but wonder how or why someone like Shelby would get involved in this type of illegal activity. He seemed to have everything including a beautiful wife and a son and daughter who were both doing excellent work in college. He had a home in an upscale part of Memphis and his business seemed to be doing alright. Sanders decided it must be true---the more you have the more you want.

"Mr. Sanders, Mr. Shelby will see you now. Please follow me," said the secretary.

Sanders got up and followed her back to a very large office. Shelby met them at the door and asked the secretary to hold his calls. Shaking Sanders' hand, he invited him to come in take a seat.

"Mr. Sanders, I understand you're from Memphis Press. How can I help you today?"

Typical of Sanders, he didn't beat around the bush. "I'm here to find out how you got the case of "money laundering" against you dropped. I understand the Department of Justice had a good chance of convicting you."

Shelby was not use to anyone being that blunt with him. His face turned red and he answered, "I don't know where you get your information, but you're wrong. Dover had it in for me. After he was shot and the department took another look at my case, they all agreed with me."

"Then you're glad Dover got shot?"

"Don't put words in my mouth. I did not say that," responded Shelby.

The rest of the conversation was a back and forth between Sanders and Shelby. When Sanders left his office he thanked Shelby for his time. There was no doubt in his mind that Shelby could have hired the hit-man. He knew for sure that Shelby didn't like Pete.

Chapter Twenty One

Helena
Party Time
June 30-July 1

Ruby was excited. In a short while she would be at the Big Island dance. She was expecting Mike to pick her up at any moment. Oh, how she loved to dance, but tonight was going to be different. Mike was a good dancer; in fact Mike was good at everything. However, she had decided to dedicate tonight to Joe Cole. It would take all her womanly charm to get under his skin and she had to do it without Mike getting jealous.

Pete and Ruby were convinced they had a pretty good handle on the small people in the drug ring. They even knew some of the middle people. They had the evidence on the loaders and drivers and the people who paid Mike for the drugs, even the ones in Chicago.

She had heard Mike telling his dad how good the trip to Chicago went. He didn't know that when the trooper stopped Vic's truck, he attached a tracking device to the underside of the truck. That device had allowed the FBI to follow Vic's truck into Chicago and the warehouse where it was unloaded. They had good picture evidence of both trucks being unloaded as well as the transfer of money to Mike.

Now, Mike was at the door with a single red rose in his hand. "For you," he said with a smile.

"I could get use to this," responded Ruby. "You want a drink or anything before we go?"

"Beside the drink, what are my choices?" teased Mike.

"I think we've better leave. I'm looking forward to the dance," answered Ruby.

+++++

The dance was in full swing by the time Mike and Ruby arrived. They found the table where Cole, Castle and Mike's dad were sitting and joined them. Ruby didn't know the three young women at the table, so Mike's dad, Leon, introduced them by first names only. The blond was Susie and was with Leon. The redhead was Christy and she was with Cole. While the smallest of the three was Shirley and by the way she was hanging on to Castle, she must be with him. It was obvious that the three couples were way ahead of Mike and Ruby in the alcohol consumption. All three of the young women had low cut blouses that show most everything they had and they didn't mind rubbing it on the man next to them. "Yes, it was party time," Ruby thought.

They had been at the dance about an hour when the men decided to do some "trading partners" in dancing. As luck would have it, Ruby got paired up with Joe Cole. She knew she had to be careful and she could not out sex the other girls in front of Mike. So she decided to play the "hard to get" role. She used all her womanly charm to make Cole want her but she let him know she was unavailable to him.

Ruby was actually having a good time when the men decided it was time to "trade partners" again. This time Ruby was paired up with Castle who had come on to her on another occasion. At that time she decided that Castle was just a harmless dirty old man, but tonight she wasn't too sure he was harmless. He acted more like a horny old man eager to prove he wasn't too old.

When it was getting late and everyone was dancing, Ruby had to go to the ladies room. On the way back to the table, she ran into Joe Cole who was headed to the men's room. While they were still out of sight of their table, he pulled her aside and kissed her before she could stop him. When the kiss was over he said, "I going to Memphis tomorrow for a meeting Monday morning. What about meeting me for dinner and whatever?"

Ruby knew what "whatever" meant. However, in spite of that she said she would meet him. He said, "I'm going to be staying at Four Points by Sheraton. Maybe you could meet me there at 7:00 p.m. and we could go to dinner from there."

"I can do that," said Ruby. "Where is it located?"

"At 5877 East Poplar Ave."

"I'd better go before Mike comes looking for me," Ruby said as she walked away.

+++++

The only time Sanders could get an appointment with Charles Schuler was 2:00 p.m. Sunday. His office was in the back of one of the nicer strip joints at 3691 Winchester. There were several security types standing around guarding Charles Schuler. Sanders was unarmed except for his small ankle weapon. He knew all of the body guards standing around had a good size weapon under their coat. It was enough to make him nervous.

One of the security people led Sanders to Schuler's office. Schuler was sitting behind a large desk smoking a large cigar, looking like a crime boss. "Sit down," he almost shouted as Sanders walked into the office. Sanders sat down and Schuler asked, "Now what can I do for you?"

Sanders knew he had to be careful or he could get carried out of this place. He said, "Mr. Schuler, I'm Sanders and I work for the Dover Detective Agency. We are investigating the murder of Janie Albert and the attempted murder of Pete Dover. Since Mr. Dover was handling your trial I wanted to ask you a few questions."

"I didn't have nothing to do with any of that. The Department of Justice still has my trial scheduled. You need to talk with Shelby. He is the one who got his case dropped after that shooting. Just ask my guys, I was here the night of the shooting."

"Mr. Schuler, the shooting was a contract killing. You could have been here and still ordered the hit."

"Wasn't me is all I got to say."

Sanders was becoming very uncomfortable and after a few more questions decided it was time for him to leave.

+++++

It was after 3:00 a.m. before Mike left Ruby's apartment. The dance had been good, she had fun. She was able to make a connection with Joe Cole. Best of all, the sex with Mike had been more than wonderful. Now it was 2:00 p.m. and she had just got up.

After a shower and some breakfast, she called Pete. She told him about her night and how the "trading partners" plan the men used actually worked to her advantage. By dancing with Joe Cole she was able to get his attention. "I have a date to meet him at Four Points by Sheraton in Memphis at 7:00 p.m. tonight for dinner and whatever."

"I don't know how you do it," responded Pete.

"Do what?"

"Go to bed with whomever or whenever, to get the information you need."

"Pete, it's hard for a woman to make it in this business. I decided early on that I had to use everything I had to do my job and sometimes, like with Mike, I actually enjoy it. However, I'm having a hard time knowing how to handle Cole. I'm not sure I can make myself go to bed with him. I don't like the man at all."

Ruby went on to talk about the reason she called Pete. "I know that Cole has a meeting in the morning in Memphis. I am not sure where, what time or with who. It could be with the person the 'plan' called Chief. Could you alert Sanders and have him ready to follow Cole when he leaves the motel in the morning? When I can, I'll call Sanders and give him as much information as I can get."

"Sounds like a plan to me," Pete said as Ruby broke the connection.

+++++

After Pete hung up the phone, he called Sanders and gave him the information he had gotten from Ruby. However, his mind was still on the part of the conversation where Ruby told him that as an FBI agent she had to use everything she had, to do her job. Somehow Pete's mind transferred that part of the conversation to Alice.

The question became, was what Alice seemed to feel for him real or was she just doing her job? It seemed to him that their relationship had grown and he could admit he had strong feelings for her. Did she feel the same way? Pete decided if she didn't she was a damn good actress.

About that time, Alice came into Pete's office and said, "I heard you talking to Ruby, did she say anything that I need to know?"

"She's coming to Memphis tonight to have dinner with Joe Cole. There is some hope that she can begin to make a connection between Helena and Memphis. She feels she may have to sleep with Cole to get the information she needs. I just don't understand how she does it."

"Does what?"

"Use sex to get what she wants."

"Women do it all the time and sometimes it's not for nearly as noble a reason."

"Do you?"

"I'd like to say no, but if I'm being truthful I have to admit I have."

"Is that what you're doing with us?" Pete knew as soon as it came out of his mouth that he shouldn't have asked that question.

Alice's look at Pete would have killed lesser men. She opened her mouth to speak, but instead turned on her heel and walked back into her office. A few minutes later, she came back into Pete's office with her purse over her shoulder and only said, "I'm leaving for the rest of the day."

Sitting in his apartment alone, Pete couldn't get his mind on his work. He could only think about Alice. He owed her his life. He enjoyed working with her. He enjoyed looking at her and being with her. Making love to her was above fantastic. How in the hell could he accuse her of screwing him as a part of her job?

+++++

It was 7:00 p.m. when Ruby pulled into the parking lot at Four Points by Sheraton. Ruby was disturbed at how little she knew about Joe Cole. She really only knew he was a powerful attorney who lived in Phillips county. They had only made plans to meet at the motel. She didn't know if that meant he would be in the parking lot, lobby or his room. She didn't have his cell phone number or room number.

Ruby didn't find him in the parking lot or lobby, so she made her way to the desk and asked for Joe Cole's room number.

The desk clerk asked, "What is your name?"

"Ruby Shipman."

"Joe Cole's room is 756 and he is expecting you."

As Ruby made her way to the elevator and the seventh floor, she wondered what she had gotten herself into. In all the conversations she had with Mike, he had not said anything about Cole. She had yet to make up her mind about going to bed with him even though she was knocking on the door to his room.

When Cole opened the door, he was wearing an expensive robe, his hair was wet and he looked as though he had just gotten out of the shower. He said, "I'm so glad you're here, come on in and I'll fix you a drink. If I remember right you were drinking a Tom Collins last night."

Looking around, Ruby felt trapped. She had the feeling that things were going to happen that she really didn't want to happen. She said, "If you have a white wine, I had rather have that."

Walking over to the bar in the suite, Cole said, "One white wine coming up."

"Thanks," said Ruby as she took the wine from Cole.

"By the way, and I hope you don't mind, I ordered dinner from room service. I noticed you ate prime rib, baked potato and salad at the Big Island Restaurant, so that's what I ordered for us."

Ruby was floored. She certainly had not expected this. However, it did explain why Cole had just stepped out of the shower and was dressed only in a robe. Ruby would bet money he had nothing on under the robe. The only real questions left were---"is he going to want 'it' before or after dinner or maybe both times and how am I going to respond?"

Ruby decided she would try to put him off before dinner, enjoy dinner and then see what happened after dinner. She knew it was not a good plan but it was the best she could think of right now. Helping to make her plan work was a knock on the door. Cole went to the door and asked the room service person to come in and set the table.

After room service had set the table and left the room, Cole laid his plans for the evening out for Ruby to hear. He said, "Room service was a little early. I had hoped we would have more time to get to know each other, but there will plenty of time for that after dinner. We should eat while the food is hot."

+++++

Andy, Sue, Sanders, Gracie and Pete were meeting at Pete's apartment. Sam was still following Rice and Alice had not come back to Pete's since she left so abruptly this afternoon. It was another one of those "what do we do now?" moments. Now that Carol was dead, the two women needed some guidance from the agency. It was decided that beginning in the morning, the two women would investigate the law firm of Sneed, Weeks and King and that Andy would move over and help Sanders.

Around 8:00 p.m. Sanders heard his cell phone. It was a text from Ruby that he read aloud, "Sanders, I'm with Joe Cole in room 756 at the Four Points by Sheraton. Meeting at 9:00 a.m. at Sneed, Weeks and King's. Not sure yet what kind of car Cole is driving. Look for something new and expensive with Mississippi tags. More later.

Sanders explained what the text meant. Gracie looked at Sue and said, "Sue, we need to be on the inside of the Sneed, Weeks and King's building when Cole gets there. Maybe we can determine who he is meeting."

Just as the meeting was about to break up, Alice came back. Pete was surprised because she acted as though nothing had happened. She said she had needed a break and had gone to a movie.

+++++

At dinner, the food had been good and the conversation, while it was filled with sexual suggestions, had been easier than Ruby had expected. Joe Cole had turned out to be a person who was not hard to be around. Ruby had taken a "powder room" break and sent Sanders a text while Cole was fixing them an after dinner drink. She knew if she was to get any more information, she would have to sleep with him and she had decided she could. She also knew the more he drank, the more he would talk and she wanted to learn all she could during the pillow talk part of this night.

Even though Cole had drank too much, the sex wasn't bad. However, with her fake orgasm and her words of praise, Ruby made Cole believe it was the best she ever had. "I came to Memphis to see you," said Ruby. "What are you doing here?"

It just spilled out. "I'm getting together with several old classmates. We call it a class reunion and we meet three or four times a year. We all went to law school at Memphis State."

"Oh, I bet that's fun." Ruby said as she snuggled up to him.

"It's great, we have a good time and as a by product we make a little money."

Ruby knew she wasn't going to get names out of Cole, but they now knew they were former classmates and if Sanders could somehow find out who Cole was meeting with, they would be a lot closer to finding the chief. Before Cole could get horny again, Ruby whispered in his ear that she needed to leave for Helena. She said, "I've got to work tomorrow and I had better get on the road."

Grudgingly, Cole said, "Okay and maybe we need to keep this little encounter a secret. Maybe that way, we can do it again sometime."

Chapter Twenty Two

Memphis
Class Reunion
July 2

Gracie had entered the Sneed, Weeks and King building at 8:30 a.m. and gone directly to the reception desk. "I'm Gracie Sanders and I'm here to see Mr. Sneed," she said.

The receptionist looked at her appointment book and said, "Do you have an appointment? I don't find your name in my book."

"Oh yes, I have an appointment for 8:45. I'm a little early."

The receptionist looked again at her book and said, "If you'll have a seat, I'll check it out."

As the receptionist was checking it out, Sue had entered the building and came to the desk. "I'm here to see Bob Wilkins. I don't have an appointment, but I was hoping that you could work me in."

"If you'll give me a little time, I'll see what I can do."

Sue took a seat which was not close to Gracie. They wanted to be kept waiting so they could see who came in and gathered with Joe Cole. They had a bird's eye view.

Meanwhile, Sanders had followed Cole to the Sneed, Weeks and King building. He called Gracie to tell her that Joe Cole was wearing a gray suit and was entering the front doors. Gracie said, "I see him."

Sanders said, "Gracie, use the camera on your phone to take pictures of anyone talking to Cole. Try not to be seen. If you see them go into a room together, if possible, get all their pictures. Since Pete worked here he should be able to identify most of the people."

Gracie responded, "I'm watching Cole. He seems to be well known among most people here. Now, he is going into a large conference room on my right. I got to go." Gracie looked like she was texting when she was really taking pictures. Sue could see what she was doing and joined in the effort.

The receptionist called Sue and Gracie to her desk. She said, "Both Mr. Sneed and Mr. Wilkins are in a meeting. They told me it would last at least an hour, but that you should feel free to wait."

Both the women decided to wait and this time when they walked back to their chairs, they sat together. Gracie called Sanders back and told him what was going on. "There were a total of eight people that went into the meeting. Both Wilkins and Sneed are in the meeting with Cole. They told the receptionist it would last over an hour, but that we were welcome to wait. We're waiting."

+++++

Ruby was at work at the Ford Dealership. Sales were slow and she had been gone several days, so she had a lot of catch-up work to do. She had called four people, who had shown some interest in trading cars, without any luck. Her phone rang and she hoped it was one of her customers calling back. However, it was Mike.

"What are you doing?" he asked.

"Trying to make a living. After all I've missed some work because of you."

"Sorry about that," he said. "Can you take a two hour lunch? I'd like to take you to Big Island."

Ruby knew her boss wouldn't like it but she might pick up some valuable information with Mike at Big Island. She said, "Pick me up in ten minutes." She closed her phone and went to tell her boss that she was taking a two hour lunch.

"Maybe you'll see someone to sell a car to while you're gone," he said.

As soon as she left the boss's office, she saw Mike pull up in front. She was excited to see him and almost ran to get in his truck. Mike had very little to say on the way to Big Island. She wondered what was on his mind and she hoped and prayed that he knew nothing of her trip to Memphis. She said, "I'm so glad to see you today, I've missed you. What's on your mind, you seem to be so quiet."

"I was just wondering where you were last night. I went by your apartment and you were not there. I called a couple of times and you didn't answer."

Ruby knew he had tried to call, but she couldn't answer and he didn't leave a message. She said, "I went to Wolf Chase Mall to do some shopping and didn't get home until late. The battery on my phone went dead and I had forgotten my charger. I'm sorry, maybe I should have let you know, but I didn't know I was supposed to answer to you."

+++++

As the class reunion group was breaking up, Gracie could hear parts of a conversation. It seemed the meeting was all about money. Their investments were paying off and everyone was excited about it. Gracie listened intently, but she couldn't make out anything about murder or drugs. It could have been simply an investment club meeting.

Two of the men stopped at the receptionist's desk to talk to her. Bob Wilkins was the first to face the women. Mrs. Sue Dover, I'm sorry to have kept you waiting so long. Would you come this way? As Sue followed Wilkins she remembered Stan saying how much the place reminded him of "old money".

After an extended conversation with the secretary, Mr. Ed Sneed invited Gracie to his office. Gracie was impressed with the appearance of the office and as she started to sit down, heard Sneed say, "Mrs. Dover, please sat down. I am sure whatever you want to see me about is important, so let get to it."

"I am here investigating the murder of one of your employees and the attempted murder of my son."

"Both your husband, Andy, and your father in law, Stan, have been here and have talked with Donald Weeks and Bob Wilkins. I'm sure I wouldn't have anything to add to what they have already said."

Sue felt the same bush-off that Andy had told her about. Something was going on and Sue felt it had something to do with the meeting she had witnessed. "I hope you do," said Sue. "You could begin by telling me about the meeting that just broke up."

"I'm sorry, I can't do that. It was a confidential meeting and I simply can't share any of that information."

"It sounded like an investment club that had just gotten a good report on their investments."

"I'm not free to confirm or deny anything about the meeting." Standing up, Sneed said, "I'm afraid that's all the time I have for you today, Mrs. Dover. After all you didn't have an appointment."

Sue knew she wasn't about to get any information from Sneed. She and Gracie had accomplished their purpose by getting pictures of everyone in the meeting with Joe Cole. She stood and said, "Mr. Sneed, I recognize a brush-off when I see one, but I do want to thank you for your time. You may never know how much you have helped."

+++++

Lunch at the Big Island Restaurant was something extra for Ruby. Mike had finally gotten over his mad spell and they were enjoying their meal when Frank Castle and Leon Wesson came in and joined them. Even though they spoke to Ruby, they talked like she wasn't there. The conversation concerned the delivery of a large load of marijuana that was coming up the river on a barge.

The marijuana had been loaded on the barge in New Orleans and had slowly made its way upriver. It would arrive on July 5th and would be the largest shipment they had ever received. The marijuana would be packaged cellophane, commingled with other products being shipped upriver.

Leon said, "Son, I want you and Vic each to get a boat and approach the barge before daylight on Thursday, load the pot in your boats and bring it back to the Pawn Shop warehouse. I'll let you know the exact time later."

Mike knew that once they unloaded in the warehouse, the operation was pretty safe. No one bothered anything on Big Island. When he was younger, he had worked in the warehouse breaking down the larger packages into smaller bags for delivery. It had been so much a part of his way of life that he didn't feel he was doing anything illegal or even wrong. They used to grow marijuana commingled with other crops, but in the last few years it had become more cost effective to buy in large amounts, have it shipped in and break it down into small bags before selling.

The conversation was dying down as Ruby said, "Mike I only have a two hour lunch hour, we had better get back." Ruby had appeared not to be interested in any of this conversation; however she was taking in the whole process and filing it away in her memory. It could be very important when the Department of Justice started wrapping up the entire case.

Chapter Twenty Three

Memphis
School Mates
July 3

Andy decided that all the Dover Detective Agency needed to meet all together and called Pete to see if they could meet at his office. He wanted Pete to call everyone and set it up for 10:00 a.m. tomorrow, July 3rd. He had been away from the case for a couple of days and was anxious to find out what the others had learned during his absence. He arrived at Pete's early and was quick to notice that Alice and Pete were in a very good mood. He could see the attraction sparks flying between the two of them. He really couldn't figure it out. The last time he was here it was like a hate relationship. Today it was more like a love relationship. Maybe they were falling in love and didn't know if they wanted to or not.

The other members of the family drifted in as Alice served them coffee and cake. After fifteen minutes of general conversation about Stan and his health issues, Andy called the meeting to order. He said, "Since I have been in Jonesboro with mom and dad for a couple of days, I want you to catch me up with the investigation. However, first let me tell you, Dad's problems came on real sudden. Mom took him to the hospital and his heart doctor put in two stents yesterday. Mom and Dad know you all wanted to be there, but they felt it was more important to find the person who tried to kill Pete. The doctors have every reason to believe that he will be as good as new in a few days.

Now, Sam, do you want to report first?"

Sam said, "I'm glad to hear that dad's okay and since I'm new to this investigation, I'd like to report last. That way, maybe some of what I have been doing will fit in somewhere."

Pete seemed to want to report for almost everyone. "I believe some things are beginning to come together. Sanders has learned that Bob Wilkins and Joe Cole went to law school together here in Memphis. That information made us pay attention when Ruby learned that Joe Cole had a meeting here in Memphis at the law firm of Sneed, Weeks and King. Sanders followed Cole and indeed he did go to the law firm. Since Sanders was known in the law firm, he waited in the car for him to come out of the building."

"Since we knew he was coming to the law firm, Sue and Gracie were already inside waiting to see Sneed and Wilkins. They had been told that both men had a meeting, but they would see them after the meeting was over. They watched as Cole, Wilkins and Sneed joined five others in the conference room. The meeting lasted an hour and when the meeting broke up, Sue and Gracie were able to get everyone's picture with their cell phone."

Three of the pictures included people they all knew: Joe Cole, Bob Wilkins and Ed Sneed. Pete identified two of the other pictures as Jeremy Sides and Alonzo Harris. They were both lawyers who worked for Sneed, Weeks and King. All five of the men looked to be about the same age. That still left three men that needed to be identified.

Sanders had two ideas where he needed help. First, he hoped that Schuler or Shelby would be a part of the group, they were not there. Second, Sue and Gracie said they heard nothing that indicated this group had anything to do with Operation Delta Pride. He said, "I believe their words were, 'it could have been a meeting of an investment club.' Do we have any evidence that it was more than that?"

Sue responded, "You are right; we did say it could have been an investment club meeting, however we followed three of the men, Cole, Wilkins and Sneed as they left the law firm building. They had lunch with a fifth man that Gracie and I didn't know and we weren't able to get his picture. We had lunch at a table close to them and overheard them talking about a large delivery of marijuana coming upriver soon. They were already counting their money."

"I never saw the fifth man," said Sanders.

Suddenly, Pete jumped in, "Ruby called me last night about a large shipment coming upriver before daylight on July 5th. I wonder if that is the same shipment and since Cole is a part of both groups, I bet it is."

"I'm new to this investigation, so this may be off the wall, but what would happen if we had it confiscated," asked Sam.

Several ideas were voiced.

"It would alert the drug ring."

"It would shake things up."

"It would give us some people to interrogate for more information."

"Let me think about it, it may be a good idea," said Pete. "If we could get someone on the inside to turn states' evidence, it could go a long way in identifying the chief. I feel like Witcher would approve the idea."

It had been a long meeting, but Pete felt it had been productive. Sue and Gracie were to find out who the other three men in the meeting of eight were. They also had hopes of finding the fifth man who had lunch with Cole, Wilkins and Sneed.

"I know we have been here a while, but I need you to help me sort out what I have been doing," said Sam.

"We're good at sorting out," said Gracie.

"Okay, my issue is Rick Rice. For a man to be in a long term relationship, he sure acted suspicious. He almost never went to see Carol, and yet he went to dinner with Anita Knox and later went to her apartment and spent the night. The next day Carol died. After taking care of the details with the hospital, he spent the night with Knox again. The next morning, he left for Atlanta."

"Anita Knox worked the day shift in ICU. She was there when Carol died," Sue spoke up. "I can't help but wonder what that means. Sam, it won't make anything more clear, but Carol was deathly afraid of Rice. She didn't want to be alone with him. He didn't come to see her often because she didn't want to see him."

"I met Knox one day when I was at the hospital. She is a nice looking person, but you know, she could have done it. I've had a nagging suspicion that Carol was murdered," responded Sanders.

Andy spoke up, "Sanders, since you know who Knox is, I want you to do a complete workup on who she is and what's going on in her life."

+++++

Over the years Sue and Gracie had developed a strong relationship and they had come to enjoy working together. Even their over-protective husbands liked it. The men had always been nervous about sending them out on dangerous jobs by themselves; however somehow, if they went together, it seemed safer.

There was really nothing dangerous about today's assignment. They were at the University of Memphis library trying to find names to go with the three pictures that no one could identify. It might have been easier to go back to Sneed, Weeks and King's and ask a secretary, but that would have alerted them and they probably wouldn't have been given the information they wanted anyway. From the records office at the college, they had discovered Wilkins, Sneed, Cole, Harris, and Sides had all been students from 1991 to 1996. Now they were at the library looking through the school yearbooks for those years.

Gracie was the first to find her man. His name is Cleo McFadden, she almost shouted and in a quiet library you don't do that. He graduated in 1995. Gracie looked to Sue and said, "I'm going to 'google' him and see what I find."

"I'll keep looking," said Sue.

Gracie put Cleo McFadden, 1995 graduate of University of Memphis Law School into "google" and waited for what seemed like forever. The search even brought up a picture, along with some new information. Cleo had been working as an attorney for Sneed, Weeks and King for twelve years. He lived at 1116 Almetta Dr, in Collierville. He was married to the former Jane Carter and they had two sons. Gracie printed off her information just as Sue was sitting down to a computer.

"We just lack one," said Sue. "I found a J W Bryan who graduated in 1994."

"I'll go back and look for the third person, while you look up your man," responded Gracie.

It took some time, but finally Sue found J W Bryan. As she took her information around to Gracie, Gracie asked, "What took you so long?"

"Well there was a problem. Under J W Bryan, the only thing I learned was that he graduated from University of Memphis law school in 1994. After that, he seemed to have disappeared. I was stumped. Then I got lucky. I asked the computer for variations of the name, J W Bryan. It gave me, what seemed like, hundreds of names. I decided to start at the bottom of the list and the fifth one up was J Weston Bryan."

According to the printed information, including his picture, J Weston Bryan was indeed their man. He had also worked for Sneed, Weeks and King for seven years. Bryan lived in Germantown at 18817 Hydrick Road. He is married to a Sherry Waldrep-Bryan and they have three girls.

Sue and Gracie continued to look for the eighth man, but were having no luck. They knew there were some pictures of students which were not in the yearbooks and they had to assume he was one of them. They knew in their heart that he was a classmate of the other seven. In fact, they believed the man at the restaurant was also a classmate. They had to find a way to discover his identity. Maybe they could ask Daisy to search the internet for the identity of the man in the picture.

+++++

Daisy wasn't too happy with the situation with Sam being in Atlanta. She had two small children to take care of all alone and besides that, she missed her husband. However, she knew it was necessary and she had to live with it.

Andy had assigned Sam the job of finding out any and everything he could about Rick Rice. In order to do his job, it was necessary to go to Atlanta. He began by making sure Rice was not at home. Then he began to interview Rice's neighbors.

Sam began by going up the street north. As he went north, he worked four houses on the east side of the street and came back on the west side. He continued working south on the west side then crossed the street and worked back to Rice's house on the east side. Sam had talked with nine people and heard a consistent response. No one knew Carol had died. Each of the neighbors told Sam, they really didn't know Rice or Carol. They almost never saw them outside and they seemed to be out of town a lot. No one knew where Rice or Carol worked, but some of the neighbors thought they must have their own business somewhere.

Without making any headway, Sam wondered what his next step should be. He missed his wife and decided to call her. She answered on the second ring. The caller ID told Daisy who was calling. "Hello, I love you more. Why don't you come over, my husband is out of town," she teased.

"I'm out of town too. Could I be the husband you're talking about? I can't be there for a few days, but I miss you terribly."

"Me too. Are you having any luck?"

"Not yet, but I have hopes. I have interviewed the neighbors and learned very little. I plan to be at his house before daylight in the morning and follow him. I hope he leads me to his business or place of employment."

"I just talked to Gracie and she told me they had identified three of the other men in the meeting at Sneed, Weeks and King. It seems they got their names through their college yearbooks and once they had a name, they googled it, and got more information as to where they lived and worked. All three of them worked at Sneed, Weeks and King. I wondered if I might help you by trying to find Rice on the computer."

Sam replied, "It sure couldn't hurt any. Call me if you learn anything."

+++++

Sanders began his background work-up on Anita Knox by going to the personnel office of the hospital. From her records, the HR director told Sanders Anita is 34 years old. She has been a nurse for eleven years and has worked for the hospital for six years. She has been in the ICU unit for three years. Anita is considered a good employee. She is not married and has no children. She lives in apartment 17 at 2364 Perkins Road.

From her apartment manager, Sanders found out Anita was responsible with her rent, but was also somewhat on the wild side. It was not uncommon for her lights to be on, and the noise to be loud coming from her apartment, well into the morning hours. The neighbors added, she had a dare-devil type personality. There wasn't anything she was not willing to try at least once.

Finally, Sanders learned she was having money problems. Her credit rating was considered fair-to-good. She had five credit cards which were all maxed out. Her car payment was thirty days past due. In the past, she had been making one payment just before the next one was due.

Sanders needed one more piece of information before he formed an opinion. He wanted to see Carol's doctor. Luckily for Sanders, Dr. Julie Imboden was finishing rounds in the ICU when he caught up to her. She said, "Follow me to my office; I have a few minutes now."

Sanders followed the fifty something year old, slightly overweight doctor to her office. The office was bare, with only a desk and desk chair plus two other chairs for others. "Please sit down, Mr. Sanders. I know your concern is Carol Wooten, who died Saturday in our ICU. How can I help you?"

"I don't know how much you know about Carol; so, let me give you a quick rundown. She was a hired killer who killed Janie Albert and tried to kill Pete Dover twice. In her second attempt, she was shot by an FBI agent who was protecting Pete. We were afraid someone would try to kill her before she could tell us who hired her."

"I'm up to date on most of that information. My question is, what do you need from me?"

"Dr. Imboden, is it possible that Carol did not die as a result of the FBI gunshot that came several days ago?"

"I have wondered about the same question. Carol seemed to be responding to treatment and I had expected her to live. My major concern had become her ability to communicate. So it is easy to answer your question, yes, it's possible. However, the truth is, I can't say, with certainty, what caused Carol Wooten to die."

"What does your gut tell you?"

"If you force me to guess, I'd say there was a 70—30 chance she was murdered. However, I wouldn't say that in a court of law."

+++++

Al was sitting at their normal table waiting for Sally to set down her Southwest plane from Dallas. Even though they had been watching the baggage handlers religiously, they had not learned anything new. It had become normal for the handlers to load the last baggage from the plane on the train and to take it to the enclosed area in the old hanger building.

Normal seemed to be the word for today. Al's love life also seemed to be progressing normally. Oh, there was nothing wrong that he could put his finger on, but there was also no excitement. Just normal--the same old thing--day after day. He really didn't know what he expected, but he knew he wanted more than this.

Even his job had taken on a "same old" feeling. All he did was direct planes as they left and approached the airport. While it was true, the job was pressure packed. Al had allowed it to become routine.

He remembered what someone had told him a long time ago. "Get down off the cross, someone needs the wood." He had to admit he was feeling sorry for himself. He was on his pity-pot. He needed some excitement in his life.

Just as Sally's plane set down on the runway, a tire or tires blew and the plane was thrown off the runway and came to rest upside down in the grass. Al shot out of his chair and toward the plane, just as runway workers, fire trucks and other equipment begin to show up.

Chapter Twenty Four

Memphis—Helena
The Raid
July 4

    The fire trucks had foamed down the plane. The danger of fire was not as great, but the plane did have fuel leaking from one of the tanks. Six men were working to stop the leak. Al didn't know how that many people had been assembled so quickly. The main thing was to get the injured passengers off as soon as possible, and then the rest of the passengers. Finally, they had to make sure all the crew was safely out of the plane. Al was worried about Sally and then he saw her. She was helping the crew get everybody off.

    Once everybody was out and the danger of fire was over, the passengers were told their baggage would be brought to the baggage area. Someone who seemed to be in charge said, "It appears that no one was critically injured. We'll have a more complete report later. We want to ask you to be patient with us, it will take a while but we'll get everything sorted out and everything back to normal."

    When Sally walked over to Al, he hugged her and said, "I've been sitting up there at our table feeling sorry for myself and then I saw your plane run off the runway and turn upside down. Immediately everything changed. I didn't know what was going to happen next. I knew then I couldn't lose you. I love you, Sally, will you marry me?"

Sally had been calm and strong in the whole accident. She did what she had been trained to do, didn't miss a thing, but when Al said, "I love you, will you marry me?" She threw her arms around him and began to cry a cry of joy, fear, love and excitement all wrapped into one.

"Was that a yes?" Al asked.

"YES!"

+++++

Waking up in bed with Alice was like a little piece of heaven. Still in a state of dreamland, Pete realized it was the 4th of July and here he was enjoying life to the fullest. As he turned to face her, he was still impressed with the beauty of her body. Everything was put together perfectly. He decided he could get used to this.

Suddenly he woke up fully and became aware of what this 4th of July meant. Debra Witcher had approved the raid on the marijuana coming up the river at Helena. It was time for Pete to put the plan in place. The plan called for eight additional DEA people to be present when the raid occurred. Pete and Sanders would be there as well. Pete had not yet decided what to do about Ruby. The raid would take place in less than twenty four hours. Pete slipped out of bed, dressed and went to his desk.

Pete had been cooped up in the apartment about as long as he could stand it. He had seen his doctor yesterday and he had given Pete permission to begin some activity outside. He might be stretching it a little, but he was going to be a part of this raid come hell or high water.

Pete had been working on the plan for about thirty minutes when Alice came into his office. "I don't smell the coffee," she said. "What's for breakfast?"

"Oh, honey, I'm sorry. I got so wrapped up in the plans for the raid that I forgot to make coffee. You want me to fix it now?"

"I'll take care of it. You want breakfast?"

"Please." Pete said as he picked up the phone to call Sanders and go over his plans for the raid. Pete wanted it all to go like clockwork. The two of them talked for thirty minutes while Alice was cooking breakfast. When she called Pete to announce breakfast was ready, Pete told Sanders he would have to hang up for now, but would call him again later.

During breakfast, Pete continued to think and talk about the upcoming raid. He said, "I'm getting out of this apartment today and I plan to take part in the raid tonight. What do you want to do?"

"I'm not sure you're physically able, but I know you well enough to know that you're going to do what you want to do, especially since the doctor took off some of the your restrictions. Therefore, my job in the raid will be to watch your back. The job is the same, the location will change."

+++++

As the sun came up, you could see the damage at the crash site. Things could have been a lot worst. No one had been killed and it was believed that everyone who went to the hospital was treated and sent home. Sure the plane was still upside down and the jury was still out as to whether it could be repaired, but the answer was probably not. The baggage handlers had been able to move all the baggage to the baggage area. They were concerned that there were too many people around to move the drugs that had been hidden in the secret compartment.

Investigators were everywhere. Checking the maintenance records, they found the tires that had blown to cause the crash were almost new. The first, best guess was, it was simply an accident caused by faulty tires and not human error. In their search of the plane, the investigators found the secret compartment had been broken opened in the crash. Various kinds of drugs were scattered in open view. The Drug Enforcement officers seemed to appear out of nowhere.

Since Sally had not been hurt, she had been kept at the airport all night and, of course, Al stayed with her. "What a night," she thought. "First, I crash my plane. Then I get a proposal of marriage. Finally, I get to stay at the airport answering questions all night."

+++++

Pete's phone rang before 9:00 a.m. It was Debra Witcher. The DEA officers at the airport had contacted her about the drugs found on the Dallas to Memphis plane that had crashed. "Could you have your best man go to the airport and check it out?"

Pete had heard about the crash as he was eating breakfast, so he said to Witcher, "I can do better than that. The doctor turned me loose yesterday. I'm on my way to the airport." With that statement, Pete hung up his phone.

Alice had overheard the conversation with Witcher, so, as Pete began to get up from his desk, Alice said, "I'm going with you."

"You drive while I call Mom and Sanders," responded Pete.

Pete decided to call Sanders first. He dialed the number and heard the familiar response, "Sanders."

"Sanders, they have found drugs on the plane that crashed last night. I'm going out there to meet the DEA officers who are working the case."

"Do you need me?"

"I don't think so, Alice is going with me. I just wanted to let you know where I was and that I will call you later."

"If you and Alice get a chance, come over to the house around 1:00. I'm cooking out to celebrate July 4th."

Next, Pete called his mom. "Mom, what have you heard from grandpa? I hope he is doing alright and I wanted to let you know that I'm going to the airport to talk with the DEA officers who are working the crash. They have found drugs in a secret compartment of the plane."

Sue responded, "Your grandpa is doing alright, but I think you have lost your mind." You know the doctor just released you from confinement in your apartment. You're not ready."

Pete interrupted, "Mom, I'll be careful. Love you. Bye now."

+++++

In spite of it being July 4th, Rice was leaving his house at 7:00 a.m. and Sam was following him. Sam only hoped he was going to work and not some July 4th picnic later in the day. Sam had talked with Daisy and found that she had no luck in finding a business attached to Rice's name. In order to do a complete work-up on the man, Sam needed to know what kind of legal business or job Rice had.

The traffic in Atlanta was light this July 4th. Sam assumed people must be out of town or sleeping in. Rice was parking on a street in front of a business. The sign out front said it was the "Travel Right---Travel Agency" which was open from 8:00 until 4:00 seven days a week. As Rice entered the building, he turned on the lights and turned the "closed" sign around so that it now read, "open".

Sam was parked across the street from the travel agency and decided to wait a few minutes before going inside to ask about a cruise to Mexico. While he was waiting, a young woman went into the shop. Sam could see that she sat at the desk that was located at the front window.

As Sam entered the shop, the young woman said, "Good morning, my name is Megan, how can I help you today?"

"I'm interested in a cruise to Mexico. Could you show me what is available?"

"I'd love to. Please sit down," Megan said. Almost immediately Megan was reaching across her desk to show Sam their most popular Mexico cruise. As she was explaining the package, Rice came out of the back office and was moving toward the front door.

"I'll be gone most of the morning," he said.

"Alright, but before you leave let me introduce Sam to you. He's looking at a possible cruise to Mexico." Rice came over and shook hands with Sam and told him he couldn't go wrong with the trip Megan was showing him.

Sam was faced with a problem. Should he follow Rice or should he stay here and pump the travel agent for all the information he could get from her? He made a quick decision. He decided he would learn more by talking to the secretary.

+++++

Sanders was cooking out. Gracie was there telling him how to do it, when Andy and Sue arrived. Daisy was expected, but was running late because of the kids. Sam was still in Atlanta doing work on Rice. Stan and Pat were staying in Jonesboro because Stan was still recuperating from his hospital stay. Gracie hoped that Pete and Alice would drop by as well as Al and Sally. They would miss the part of the family who were not able to be here today.

It was July 4th and it was hot in Memphis. Gracie thought it was 105 degrees outside. The TV weather man said the heat index was 112 degrees. This kind of heat meant everything but Sanders' cooking would be on the inside. It was going to be a fun break from all the anxious moments and hard work since the attempt on Pete's life.

Pete, Alice, Al and Sally arrived together. They always brought the excitement of the young, but today there was something more going on. Sally couldn't wait, she said, "What a night I've had. First, I crashed my plane. Then, I get a proposal of marriage. Finally, I get to stay at the airport answering questions all night. I am the happiest woman alive."

The women got together with their "that's wonderful, have you set the date?" to "can I see your ring?" Sally told them it all happened so quick that Al had not had time to buy the ring. They were going in the morning to pick it out.

Meanwhile, the men got a beer, went outside with Sanders and began to ask their questions. "Have they determined what caused the crash? What about the drugs found on the plane? Is everything set for the raid tonight?" That's the kind of conversation that went on until the men began to bring the food in through the back door.

By then, Daisy and her kids had arrived and the celebration continued around the dinner table and when most of the food was gone, they called Stan and Pat and told them how much they were missed. Stan was doing a little better and Pat was the wonderful caretaker she had been all their marriage.

At this moment, all was right with the world, but then it was over and it was time to get back to reality. The four DEA officers at the plane crash wanted to go on the raid with Pete. Witcher had called in four more officers. Those eight, plus Pete, Alice, Sanders and Andy were to meet at a small fishing camp, three miles south of Big Island at 6:00 a.m. Their boats were being brought in by the DEA officers. The whole group would be dressed as fishermen and the hope was that people would see them as a bunch of men who were going fishing together.

+++++

Ruby was spending July 4th with Mike. They were on Sardis Lake enjoying the water and Mike's boat. Ruby couldn't help herself, her feelings for Mike had become serious and she didn't know what to do about it. She tried not to think about it but it kept coming back.

Ruby knew about the raid that was coming before daylight tomorrow. It was all she could do not to warn Mike or at least ask him not to pick up the marijuana from the barge. However, it was her job to stay "uncover" and continue to gain information about the drug ring. She didn't know what was going to happen to her and Mike once Operation Delta Pride was over. She only knew that she had fallen in love with him.

Except for her thoughts about the raid, the day had been perfect. Because of the heat, there were not too many people on the lake and they had been able to find a deserted cove and enjoyed skinny dipping and making love. But now it was over and Mike has announced it was time for them to go. She knew what that meant, so she was very quiet on the trip back to Helena.

+++++

All five boats were in the water, the raid was beginning. Pete had decided to seize the marijuana as it was being loaded into Mike and Vic's boats. He wanted to be able to arrest the people on the barge and send a message to the drug world that barge trafficking of drugs was not safe any longer. They continued to act as though they were fishing. They didn't want to alert anyone until the very last minute.

Pete was thankful for a full moon. When they had fished down river far enough to see the barge they waited for Mike and Vic to show up. Then they saw them. Pete and two other boats were on the side of the barge that Mike and Vic approached. They had the barge surrounded, but waited until most of the marijuana had been loaded into the two smaller boats.

Sanders had warned of a shoot-out, but no one had expected the raid. No one had a gun close enough to use them. Two men had jumped from the barge, to escape in the water, but they were quickly picked up. The barge company was called and would send additional men to take over the barge. Two DEA officers were left on the barge to watch over a couple of workers until the new workers from the company arrived. The other barge workers were arrested along with Mike and Vic and their boats, loaded with marijuana, was seized. Just as quickly as the raid had begun, it was over. It took no longer that one hour.

+++++

Leon Wesson was waiting at the Pawn Shop for Mike and Vic. He had sent two men down to the river to help them unload the marijuana. They too were waiting. From their view of the river, they couldn't see the raid taking place. An hour went by, then two. It was almost daylight. Where could they be? Wesson got in his pickup and drove up the river levee. He could see the barge and everything looked normal. But where were Mike and Vic?

Wesson drove on up river to the fishing camp. People were outside cooking breakfast and talking to each other in groups. When Wesson got out and walked up to the fishermen, he could hear them talking about DEA officers and a raid they had just conducted. When Wesson asked about it, one fisherman said, "They got more marijuana than I had ever seen before. Two large bass boats full. Must have been twenty five officers. They arrested six men that I saw. It must have come off that barge."

From the information he got at the fishing camp, Wesson could put it together. If the DEA was involved, Mike, Vic and the others were on their way to Memphis. "But how did they know where and when to do the raid?" he thought. As he drove away from the camp, he called Joe Cole and said, "Get the hell up, we've got big trouble."

+++++

Sam's choice to stay at the travel agency and pump the secretary for information had been a good one. She had flirted with him---he had flirted with her, and she loved to talk. Megan said, "Carol Wooten actually owned the agency. She's the one who hired me and I've been working here for three years. I heard she got shot trying to kill some lawyer for money. I have to say I wasn't too surprised. About two years ago, things began to change. Rice began to come to the shop more since Carol was gone a lot.

Sam had set the stage and returned the next morning about 9:00. Rice was not there and Megan seemed not to know or care where he was. Sam had decided it was time to tell Megan that he was a detective who worked for the Dover Detective Agency in Memphis. He was in Atlanta investigating the attempted murder of Pete Dover, his nephew. "What can you tell me about Rice?" he asked.

"I can tell you he is not the boss that Carol was. He didn't seem to care what was happening here. His mind was always somewhere else. He was on the phone a lot. Many times he was talking to someone he called, 'Chief'."

The word chief got Sam's attention. He asked, "Do you have the chief's phone number?"

"I may have. The phone bill just came in and I think I will recognize it when I see it." Megan opened a drawer and pulled the phone bill. As she looked at it, she said, "There's the number. It's 910-667-8856."

As Sam wrote down the number, Megan asked, "Do you believe Rice is involved?"

"Let me put it this way. If I were you, I'd be careful and I'd start looking for a new job.

+++++

Pete was in the Shelby County jail interrogating Mike Wesson before his lawyer could get there. Up to this point Mike had said absolutely nothing. Sanders and Ruby were on the other side of the glass, looking at the interrogation. Ruby had just come back from the restroom and said, "I don't feel so good this morning."

"What's going on?"

"I'm sick to my stomach, but if it's like yesterday, it should go away in about an hour."

Teasingly, Sanders said, "Maybe you're pregnant."

"God no!" said Ruby. "Although I have been exposed." Ruby thought about it a minute and said, "I can't be pregnant, not now. I know I love the guy, but the trouble he's in would make life with him impossible." As Ruby was thinking over her situation, she saw Leon Wesson and Joe Cole walking down the hall. Quickly she ducked back into the restroom, but she wasn't sure if they had seen her.

Wesson and Cole had come to the jail to get Mike and Vic out and/or to make sure they didn't talk. Cole would be with Mike on all interrogations from now on. On the way to Memphis they had asked themselves the question, "How did the Feds know the marijuana would be unloaded at just that time and place?"

They didn't believe anyone in Phillips County knew it was happening. Cole said, "We've got most of the county shut so tight that even if they knew, they wouldn't talk."

After some time of trying one option and then another, Wesson said, "Damn fire, it's the girl!"

"What girl?" asked Cole.

"Mike's girl, Ruby! It has to be her. I'll be a son of a bitch. I'm going to have her killed!"

Cole was remembering the night he had spent with Ruby and how she had pumped him about his meeting at Sneed, Weeks and King. He said, "As bad as I hate to admit it, you may be right."

When it was safe, Ruby had come out of the restroom and told Sanders she had to take care of something. As she was leaving the jail she thought, "I have to know now. Maybe a pregnancy test will tell me something."

Chapter Twenty Five

Memphis
Closing In
July 6

Pete was able to keep Mike and Vic in custody, but he was not able to get any information from them. For their plan to identify the chief to succeed, someone had to talk. He also was not able to keep Cole and Wesson away from them.

Cole, Wesson and Mike were now in a sort of visitation room. Mike was angry. He wasn't sure who he was mad at, but someone was responsible for him sitting in this jail. He wanted to know who and he wanted Cole or his dad to tell him how it happened.

Wesson said, "Son, I believe Cole and I have it figured out and we will take care of it. You remember a few days ago when you and Ruby were at the Big Island Restaurant and we joined you."

"Sure, but what's that got to do with it?"

"If you remember we were pretty open with our plans for getting the marijuana from the barge to the Pawn Shop."

"I remember."

"The loose end has to be Ruby. We've looked at this every way we can and each time it comes up, Ruby is working for the other side." Very slowly and deliberately, Wesson said, "Son, I'm having her killed."

As Cole and Wesson left, Cole encouraged Mike to keep calm and not to talk. "It's going to take some time but we'll get this whole thing worked out."

Sitting alone, waiting for whatever was coming next, Mike had time to think. Ruby had become very important to him. He almost went nuts Sunday night when he didn't know where she was and couldn't find her. If he was honest with himself, he guessed he could say he was in love with her. Now this---and his dad was going to have her killed. Mike knew his dad and knew he would get it done.

+++++

Andy, Sanders, Ruby, Alice and Pete went to the Dover Detective Agency conference room to try to determine their next move. Gracie and Sue had come to the office this morning, so they joined the others in the conference room.

"Pete, can you bring us all up to date as to where we are right now on the raid?" asked Andy.

"That's easy. The raid went perfect, but the purpose was a failure."

"I don't understand," said Gracie.

"What I mean by my 'smart ass' remark was simply we were able to seize the marijuana and arrest those responsible. However, we had hoped someone would talk. At this point, no one has said anything helpful in identifying the chief. Now that Mike's lawyer is involved, it's going to be really hard to make that happen."

Ruby spoke up. "I have a question and a suggestion. Let me begin with the question. I don't know if Cole and Wesson saw me at the jail earlier this morning but I was already nervous of them figuring out that I was the informant---what do I do now?"

Gracie looked at her husband, Sanders, and noticed the way he was looking at Ruby. Gracie couldn't help but remember that her husband used to date Ruby back when they were both in the FBI in New Orleans. In spite of those issues, she said, "Ruby, we have to get you out now." The rest of the Dover's agreed and Ruby was relieved.

Pete said, "I'll work the details out with your boss in New Orleans. In the meantime, for your safety don't go back to Helena. I want you to stay in Memphis and help us."

"Thank you for that. Now, I do have a suggestion. If the Department of Justice could offer to drop the charges and to put Mike in the witness protection plan in exchange for his testimony, he might be willing."

"That would mean he would have to testify against his father. That's a lot of loyalty to turn your back on. I don't believe he would do it," responded Andy.

"Dad, I'm inclined to agree with you, but you never know until you try," added Pete.

The debate about offering the deal to Mike went on until Ruby said, "Mike doesn't know this, but I just found out I am carrying his child." You could have heard a pin drop. Ruby went on, "If Mike is willing to take the deal, I would be willing to retire from the FBI and go with him as husband and wife."

"When do you plan to tell Mike?" asked Pete.

"I don't know, I just found out about thirty minutes ago when I took the pregnancy test. I've had morning sickness the last two mornings."

Gracie and Sue said, "That was the tell-tale sign for me."

Sanders said, "This puts a new slant on the whole thing with Mike. If and when you tell him he will have a divided loyalty between his dad and his child. I'm not sure what he will do with that but it is sure worth a try."

"Ruby, don't do anything until I talk with Witcher. If she gives me the go ahead, you have my vote and support," responded Pete.

The office phone rang as the meeting was breaking up. It was Sam and he wanted to talk to Andy. "I'm on my way back to Memphis," Sam said. "I believe I have the phone number for the chief. If you have a pencil I'll give it to you."

"Okay, I'm ready," said Andy.

"It's 910-667-8856. I haven't called the number because I was afraid I might scare him off. See if you can find out who owns that number. I've called Daisy and told her I would be home in about six hours. See you then."

"Pete, can you get Homeland Security to listen in on 910-667-8856. Sam's thinks the number belongs to the chief. Homeland Security could tell us who owns the number and listen to the conversation. If it sounds like someone trying to contract with a hit-man to have someone killed, we know we got the right person." said Andy.

+++++

Pete was totally wiped out. On his first day after being released from the apartment, he had investigated drugs found on the plane that had crashed at the airport and spent the night on the Mississippi River on a raid. He felt dirty and needed a shower and a change of clothes. He said, "Alice, take me home."

"And, boy, was the shower feeling good," he thought as the water ran off his soapy hair on its way to the floor. He was startled when he heard the shower door open, but he quickly relaxed when he felt her tender fingers massaging his shoulders and washing his back. He could feel his energy level rising as Alice continued to massage his body. When he had gotten the soap out of his eyes, he turned to face Alice and returned the favor.

Much later, they were still lying in bed, when Alice voiced her concern. "Now that the case seems to be wrapping up, what should I do?"

"What do you mean?"

"I mean, do I go out and look for an apartment, now that you don't need a body guard? I mean, Pete, what about us?"

Pete responded, "There is still a lot of work to do. We don't know who hired Carol to kill me. I will need you close to me for the foreseeable future."

"And what about us?" Alice asked when it was obvious that Pete wasn't dealing with that question.

Knowing he was going to have to answer the question honestly, Pete said, "Honey, I like it the way things are now. I'm just not ready to move to the next level. Maybe after the case is solved we can talk about it more and I can make a better decision."

With a half serious and half tease tone in her voice, Alice said, "I know now, I should have asked that last question when I stepped into the shower with you and started to wash your back."

+++++

It had been two hours since Cole and Mike's dad had left his cell. Mike had been alone with his thoughts. The whole thing was unbelievable for him. Just the fact that he had been arrested for drug trafficking seemed impossible and so was the fact that he had admitted to himself that he was in love with

Ruby. The truth is she was using him to gain information for the Feds. Now, his dad was going to kill her.

Mike's mind and emotions were very confused when the guard came in to take him to a visitation room. To make it worse, Ruby was sitting at a table facing the door as Mike walked into the room. It was a good thing the guard was there, Mike probably would have saved his dad the trouble of having her killed.

As Mike sat down, he said, "Are you happy now? What are you doing here? Did you come to gloat?

"No, I'm not happy and I didn't come to gloat. I came to tell you that I was just doing my job and somewhere along the way I fell in love with you."

"I don't believe that. I wonder what you could possible want from me now?"

Ruby reached across the table to take Mike's hand, but he drew it back. She said, "I have been a part of working out a deal so that you can stay out of prison. The Justice Department will put you in the witness protection program if you will turn states evidence."

"That would mean I would have to throw my dad under the bus. Why would I do that?"

Pete and Alice were watching through the glass. Pete was listening intently because the conversation between Ruby and Mike was about to get to the critical part. He had cleared the way with his boss for Ruby to offer the deal. Now, he hoped Mike would accept the deal.

"Mike, we have the evidence to put most everyone involved in drug trafficking in prison. You might as well face it; your dad is going to prison anyway. We need help with the person at the top---the chief."

Mike was furious with Ruby. She had betrayed him. "I don't think so," he said.

Ruby sat still a few minutes, thinking. She made the decision. "I only have one more thing to say. After I've said it, I don't want you to answer. I want you to think about it and get me your answer through Pete." Very hesitantly she said, "It is important for you to know, I am in love with you. I didn't mean for it to happen but it did. I believe you love me too. If you will go into the witness protection program, I will resign from the FBI and go with you." There, she had said half of it. Drawing all the courage she had she looked Mike in the eye and said, "Mike, I am carrying your child."

+++++

Wesson called the chief to get him to issue a contract hit on Ruby Shipman. He didn't like to be made a fool of and she had done it. The chief was afraid the whole thing was in danger of coming apart, so he suggested a meeting with a select part of the Classmates along with the Helena Threesome.

In the meeting, the chief said, "I don't like surprises and we have just had a major catastrophe. I called you all together to make sure everyone understood what was happening." He went over what had happened and who was responsible for the Fed's knowing when and where to conduct the raid.

He continued, "I'm going to get Rice to take out Ruby and I think it is time to get rid of Pete Dover, once and for all. He has been a thorn in our side and I'm tired of it."

After some conversation, everyone in the group agreed, so the chief made the call to Rice. When Rice answered, the chief said, "I have a new job for you. Her name is Ruby Shipman. She has been working at the Ford place in Helena, but I doubt she'll be back. I don't know where she'll be. I do know she is FBI. I, also, think it's time for you to finish the job on Pete Dover." Before he hung up the phone, he said, "Rice, don't screw up?"

+++++

Homeland Security was listening to the chief and Rice. They had yet to determine who owned the number 910-667-8856. The name they had was a false name. The owner was using every trick in the book to keep his privacy intact. However, they did gain some important information and called Pete immediately. Pete answered his phone and the caller said, "The chief has just bought two more contracts---one for you and one for Ruby. Pete be careful."

Pete, Sanders, Alice, Gracie and Ruby were having a late lunch at Perkins when the phone had rung. The conversation around the table got very quiet as they tried to listen to what was being said on the phone. They had determined it was from Homeland Security, but could not make out the rest. Each of the others were anxiously waiting when Pete hung up the phone.

Pete said, "They have not been able to determine who owns the phone."

When Pete didn't say more Sanders spoke up, "And what else did they say?"

"You have to promise me that you won't tell Mom," Pete said. "She would drive me crazy being overprotective."

"Okay, we promise. Now what else did they say?"

"They said they listened in on a phone call between Rice and the chief. The chief has put out a contract on Ruby's life and renewed the contract on mine."

"How do we keep you both safe?" asked Alice.

Gracie spoke up, "The good thing is we know Rice is the one to keep an eye on."

"That's only half true," said Sanders. "Rice is the contractor. Sometimes he does the job and sometimes he has someone else do it, like he did with Carol."

"So the hit-man could be anybody," added Alice.

"Sanders, do you think it would be safer to hide them out in some sort of 'safe house'?" asked Gracie.

Not waiting for Sanders to answer, Pete said, "There is no way I'm going to hide from these killers. I plan to do my job and put them in jail."

Ruby spoke up, "I want to find out what Mike has decided."

Sanders said, "I'm not sure it makes any difference whether we hide them or let them work in the open with someone watching their back. Do we know where Rice is now?"

"I don't think so. I'll call Sam and get him on it. He developed a friendship with Megan, Rice's travel agent; I bet he can find out from her," replied Andy.

Ruby asked, "I can't go back to my apartment in Helena. Where do I stay until this thing is over?"

Gracie looked at Sanders and said, "Ruby you're welcome to stay with us. I think the important thing is for neither of you to be alone. I'll be Ruby's body guard and Alice, can you continue to watch over Pete?"

"I can and I will actually enjoy it."

+++++

Sam was home with Daisy and the kids when Andy called to ask him if he had any idea where Rice was. When Andy told him about the contracts to kill Pete and Ruby, he said he would do what he could to find him. After telling Daisy what was happening, Sam called Megan in Atlanta. Megan was at work at the travel agency and she was alone. After the polite hellos, Sam asked, "Do you know where Rice is? I have reason to believe there will be another attempt on Pete's life and it would really be nice know Rice's location."

Megan answered, "He came by here about an hour ago and told me he was leaving town and would be gone for several days. I'm to keep the business open and operate it as usual."

"Do you have any idea where he was going?"

"I believe I do. He asked me to make him a reservation at the Holiday Inn on Poplar in Memphis. I made the reservation and guaranteed it with his credit card because he wouldn't be getting there before 6:00 p.m."

Sam concluded the conversation with, "Megan, I want to thank you. You may have saved someone's life."

As soon as Sam hung up the phone, he dialed Pete. "Pete, Andy told me to let you know what I found out as soon as I could. Rick Rice was in Atlanta one hour ago. That's when he left for Memphis. When he gets here, he will be staying at the Holiday Inn on Poplar."

"Thanks, Sam."

"One more thing, I'll be at the Holiday Inn waiting for Rice. If I see him when he arrives, I'll let you know."

"Thanks again."

+++++

Rice wasn't looking forward to the trip. It was a six hour drive and he was already tired. However, for his own sake he had better get to Memphis and get these hits made. His life might depend on it. At least the trip gave him time to plan the hits.

He knew nothing about Ruby Shipman except that she had been working as a sales person at the Ford dealership in Helena, Arkansas. Rice dialed information and got the dealership phone number and dialed it. From the dealership he learned that Ruby no longer worked for them and they didn't have a forwarding address for her. The only thing Rice knew to do was call the chief and see if he could locate her. He couldn't make the hit if he didn't know where she was.

Rice dialed the chief and told him he was on his way to Memphis, but he had a problem. "The problem is I don't know this Ruby Shipman woman. I don't know what she looks like and I don't know where to find her. I have called the Ford dealership and found out she no longer works there. I need you to put an information packet together for me. If you could have it left at the desk at the Holiday Inn on Poplar, I would appreciate it.

After talking with the chief, Rice's mind went to Pete Dover. Carol had been his go-to person in the business and she had failed twice to kill Dover. Rice had learned through the chief that Dover's injuries had improved enough that the doctor had released him so that he could go back to work. The fact that he was now out and about should make it easier for Rice to take care of him.

Rice had decided he was going to do the Dover job himself. He had too much riding on the outcome to let someone else do it. However, he wanted to find someone else to take care of Ruby and he was wondering if Anita would do it. He called her and made a date for breakfast at 8:00 a.m. and suggested they meet at Bob's.

With the plans worked out in his mind, Rice cranked up the radio and began to sing along.

+++++

Mike didn't know what to do. He loved his dad and he didn't know how he could give evidence that would put him away, possibly for the rest of his life. While he was mad as hell for the way Ruby had used him, he still had strong feelings for her. He might even call it love. Maybe she really did love him, too. He just couldn't understand how she could love him and still betray him. It simply didn't make sense to him.

Now she throws in this new thing. Was she really carrying his child or was she tricking him into giving them the information they needed? Even if she was pregnant, she could still be using him. Would she really retire from the FBI and go into the witness protection program with him? Ruby had not mentioned marriage. Did she want to marry him and love him "til death we part" or just live with him long enough to arrest and convict all the members of the drug ring?

Mike knew he needed some answers before he could make a decision. He needed to talk to Ruby and he needed to talk to his dad. Mike got word to the jailer to get Pete Dover and Ruby Shipman to come to the jail. Mike said, "If you'll call Pete he will bring Ruby with him."

Two hours later, Pete and Ruby entered the jail and were taken to the visitation room. A short time later, Mike was brought to the room and as he spoke to both of them, it was obvious that he was going to be in charge of this meeting. Ruby could see that he was not as angry as before. "Pete, I want to talk with you and then, if I could, I'd like to talk to Ruby alone."

Pete looked at Ruby and said, "We can deal with that."

Mike wanted some assurance from Pete that the witness protection idea is a real possibility---not just something that Ruby had made up to get him to turn state's evidence in the case.

"Mike, the offer is real. I have it approved by Debra Witcher, who is head of the Department of Justice in this region. I will be glad to write in up and sign it, if that will make you feel more comfortable."

"If you can give me the signed, written agreement, then I will seriously consider it and give you an answer within a couple of days. I plan to talk to Dad before I make the final decision."

"I can do that. In fact, I may have time to write it up while you are talking with Ruby," Pete said, as he was leaving the visitation room.

Turning to Ruby, Mike said, "I'm having a hard time getting past the fact that you betrayed me. I know it was your job, but I also know that you used me and it hurts, bad."

Ruby replied, "It would have been easy for me if I hadn't fallen in love with you. When that happened, everything got complicated. It hurt me too. It still hurts because I love you so much."

"Did you really mean it when you said you would retire and go with me into the witness protection program? You didn't say anything about marriage or 'til death we part'. Do you plan for this to be a temporary or permanent arrangement?"

Ruby had been FBI most of her life. She could be hard as nails and she had sworn to herself that she wouldn't cry, but she could feel tears filling her eyes as she said, "Yes, I meant it and even though the FBI has meant a lot to me over the years---Mike, you mean more. If I could arrange things the way I would like it, we would get married 'til death do us part'. We would have a family together and live to a ripe old age with four children, sixteen grandchildren and seven great grandchildren."

"Are you really carrying my child, now?"

"Yes."

"I'm thinking about accepting their offer, but I need to know that it includes you."

"Darling, it does."

Just then, Pete came in with the agreement signed and handed it to Mike. Ruby said, "Mike, I'd be glad to sign our agreement too."

Mike said, "I'll wait until we can stand before the preacher."

Chapter Twenty Six

Memphis
Contract Hit
July 7

Anita was glad to see Rick. She had gotten to Bob's Restaurant before him and had waved to him. Then she watched him walk toward her table. The way he walked really turned her on and caused her to remember the recent night they had spent together. The fact that they were meeting for breakfast caused her to wonder what he had on his mind. Maybe it was about something she could do to make some additional money.

Rice kissed her on the cheek when he arrived at the table. "It felt good," she thought. The waitress got their orders and they began with small talk which didn't last long. Very quickly Rice asked, "I'm here today to ask you how you liked the job I gave you and to ask if you would be interested in doing more of the same kind of work for me."

Anita took a minute to think about how she was going to answer him. "I'm going to be totally honest with you," she said. "I enjoyed a certain thrill in doing the job. I know I shouldn't feel that way but I did. I also needed the money, so I might be interested in doing another job for you."

"I have never asked you about your skill with a gun. Many of the jobs require that skill and I need to know how you stack up in that department before we go any farther."

"As a young girl, I was raised on a farm. All us kids learned to shoot. Later, my ex-husband and I used to go out in the country and shoot a lot. I used to love to shoot the heads off turtles and snakes in the small ponds around here. I even entered a couple of contests. I didn't win but I scored 'expert' in both of them."

"Maybe she could do the job," Rice thought. Rice had picked up the information packet that the chief had sent to his motel desk and made a second copy of everything. "Here's a packet that tells you everything we know about Ruby Shipman. The only problem we have is that we don't know where she is. I have a couple of people working on finding that location. As soon as they let me know, I'll let you know. I expect you to take her out in twelve hour after I give you her location. Do you want the job? Can you do it?"

Just listening to Rice caused Anita to get excited. She couldn't believe she was actually looking forward to killing someone. "I want the job and I feel sure I can do it. Is the pay the same?

"The pay is the same and you have the job. I'll get back to you as soon as I can with the location."

+++++

Sam had picked up Rice when he arrived at the Holiday Inn. He now knew that he was in room fourteen. Around 7:30 a.m. Sam was watching as Rice came out of the motel. When he got in his car, Sam followed as Rice made his way to Bob's Restaurant where he had met with Anita a few days before. Now he was meeting her again. Sam couldn't figure out what was going on. If Rice had met Anita for dinner, Sam would have expected that Rice was trying to set up another sleepover, but the fact that it was 8:00 in the morning put a whole new slant on it.

Although they were not able to prove anything there was talk in the agency that Anita killed Carol. That's all it was, just talk. However, now that they were meeting again made Sam wonder if Rice was recruiting Anita to kill Pete or Ruby.

Sam called Pete on his cell and told him he had some news of the possible hit. "As you know, we believe that Rice is going to try to kill you or Ruby or both of you. I'm following Rice as we speak and we're about to drive by your apartment. It looks like he is just checking on you. Are you home now?"

"Alice and I are moving kind of slow this morning. We just finished breakfast and since my desk and files are still here, we're going to work here much of the day."

"Rice slowed down as he past your apartment. Pete, I plan to keep him in sight today, but I want you to be careful in case he gives me the slip. Oh, I almost forgot. Rice had breakfast with Anita and my gut tells me he hired her to kill either you or Ruby. If I had to guess I'd say Rice is going after you while Anita is going after Ruby. Do you know where Ruby is?"

Pete said, "Aunt Gracie asked her to stay with them until this is over. I'll call her and tell her what you suspect is about to happen."

+++++

Mike was back in the visitation room. He had asked his dad to come to the jail. He had made up his mind about the witness protection program. He planned to tell Pete everything he knew and go off into the sunset with Ruby. He wanted to be a father to their child. What he didn't want to do was tell his dad. He dreaded it. It wasn't going to be easy, but it had to be done.

He couldn't put it off any longer. Now, it was time to tell the man who had given him everything he ever wanted. "Dad has always been a good father to me in spite of the illegal drug trafficking that he used me to do," he thought.

Leon sat across the table. He had responded to the request that he come to the jail because his son wanted to talk to him. He had an idea of what Mike was going to say and the look on Mike's face confirmed his idea. Leon's fear was that his whole life was about to be destroyed.

"Dad," Mike said. "There is no doubt in my mind; the Justice Department has the evidence to put most everyone involved in jail. Dad, this includes you and me. They have offered me a way out. If I will turn states evidence, they will put me in the witness protection program. I didn't want to do it because of you, but they have convinced me that they already have all the evidence they need against you."

Leon wasn't surprised and said, "Son, if they already have everything they need, why do they need you?"

"They don't know who the chief is and they are waiting for to me to tell them."

"Then you have a problem because you don't know either. I have kept that information from you all these years."

"I'm asking you to give me that information and Dad, I'm also asking you to pull the contract on Ruby."

"Why would I do that?" asked Leon.

"Because Ruby is resigning from the FBI to marry me and go into the witness protection program with me."

"I don't believe that. Son, she is still using you."

"I thought so too, at first. Then she told me the rest of the story and I changed my mind."

"Then, you had better tell me that story," said Leon.

"Dad, Ruby is pregnant with my child. You are going to be a grandfather."

To say that Leon was surprised would be an understatement. He was shocked. He was speechless. He looked at his son and understood. Then, he got up and walked out of the jail.

+++++

"Ruby's staying with Gracie Sanders in their home at 2451 Briar in east Memphis," Rice said as he talked to Anita on the phone. "Locate yourself so you can see her as she comes out of the house---then take her out."

"I called in sick today, so I can keep watch all day."

"Anita, this is important, don't screw up," Rice said as he closed his phone.

Rice was sitting in his car, across the road from Pete's apartment. He had determined that Pete and Alice were in the apartment, but he had no idea how long he would have to wait until they came out the door. He was anxious because he had not done the preparation for either hit that he usually did. He didn't have the time. The chief had pushed him to get the jobs done as soon as possible. The fact that there had already been two misses with Pete Dover didn't help the situation at all.

+++++

Wesson didn't remember driving from Memphis back to Helena and Big Island. He was in deep thought. "What had he done to his son? How was he going to fix it?" He was going to be a grandfather, although he would probably never see his grandchild. This dominated his mind as he drove home.

The Pawn Shop was closed when Wesson got there. He wasn't sure where his employees were or why the store was closed. Going to his office, he sat down at his desk and picked up the phone to call the chief. "I want to cancel the contract on Ruby," he said.

"That may be hard to do," said the chief. It has already been sent to the hit-man. We have been waiting on her location, but now we know she is with Gracie Sanders. The hit could be taking place at any moment."

"You better get it stopped!" With that Wesson hung up the phone and took out paper and pen. He wrote the following letter to his son.

Mike,

I'm writing this to let you know how proud I am of you. You have been my pride and joy all your life. Never forget it.

I completely understand what you're about to do and I want to wish you, Ruby and my grandchild the best in life.

Mike, I know they have enough evidence, without you, to put me away for the rest of my life. I can't face that. Instead, I will take my own life as soon as I mail this letter.

I love you,

Dad

P.S. The chief of the drug ring is Robert Shelby who owns a chain of Supermarkets and was a classmate with the others.

Wesson reread the letter, folded it, put it in the envelope and sealed it. He wanted to be sure the letter got mailed to Mike at the jail, so he took it to the Post Office and dropped it in the mail slot himself.

While he was in Helena, he considered how he was going to take his life. He had always loved the river, so he drove to the river bridge and crossed over into Mississippi. Then he turned around so that he was facing Arkansas and Helena. He stopped and watched the river for thirty minutes. Then he drove to the middle of the bridge, got out of his pickup, climbed over the railing and jumped into the Mississippi River.

+++++

Homeland Security called Pete and said, "We have more activity on line 910-667-8856. An incoming call from Leon Wesson asked that the contract on Ruby Shipman be canceled. The owner of 910-667-8856 was not sure he could get it done. It had already been contracted out."

When Pete told Alice about the call, she asked, "I wonder what's going on?"

"I don't know. I do know that Mike was going to talk to his dad before he accepted our deal. Maybe Wesson was the one who took out the contract and if Mike told him about the child, maybe he canceled it. That's just a guess; I don't know anything for sure."

Pete called Sanders and asked, "Where's Ruby?"

"She and Gracie left a few minutes ago to go to the beauty shop. You know women; nothing perks them up like getting their hair and nails done. Why?"

"I just received word from Homeland Security that Mike's dad is trying to cancel the contract on Ruby. The chief was not sure whether it was too late or not."

"Sounds like the hit may take place at any time. We had better find them. They are at Regina Beauty Shop at 3451 Morningside Drive. I'll call Gracie as soon as we get off the phone," said Sanders.

When Sanders tried to call Gracie, he got only her voice mail. He said, "Gracie, be extra careful, the hit-man may be closing in on you."

Anita had watched Gracie and Ruby leave the house. She followed them until they pulled up in front of Regina Beauty Shop. Then she watched as they went into the shop. She found a good place to park so she could see the front door of the shop. She was new at this and was not sure what the best way to get the job done was, but she figured if she could be ready when they came out the front door she could finish the job.

Pete and Alice drove up in front of the beauty shop and hurriedly went into the shop where they found Gracie and Ruby totally calm and peaceful. "Aunt Gracie, why didn't you answer your phone?" shouted Pete.

"The battery is dead. Why? What's the matter?"

"We just got word that Mike's dad is trying to cancel the contract on Ruby, but it may be too late. The hit-man may be on the scene now."

All Ruby heard was that Mike's dad was trying to cancel the contract, however, Gracie heard the fear in Pete's voice and said, "Ruby, we're through with our hair, why don't we come back later and get our nails done."

They paid the operator for her work and walked toward the front door with Ruby leading the way. As they walked to their car, Pete waved to Sanders as he saw him pulling into a parking space. However, Sanders didn't see Pete. Instead he was looking at a woman with a rifle pointed out the driver's window toward Ruby. Just as the woman fired her rifle, Sanders was able to drive his car between Ruby and the woman. The bullet from the rifle slammed into the right rear door of the car---going through the car and getting lodged in the left rear door.

In less than an instant, Sanders was out of his car with his weapon pointed at the woman. "Put down the gun and get out of the car with your hands in the air," shouted Sanders.

Very slowly, the door opened, the rifle was placed on the ground and the woman put her hands in the air. The others joined Sanders with Pete picking up the rifle and Gracie saying, "My God, it Anita. She was one of Carol's nurses in ICU."

Pete called the police while Gracie moved Sanders' car out of the street. Sanders moved Anita to the sidewalk and began to question her. Anita was shaking; she was so frightened. "He made me do it. I've never done this before," was about all she would say. However, before the police arrived, she did confirm that Rice had hired her to kill Ruby.

When the police finally got there, Pete said, "Take her to county and book her for attempted murder. I plan to fill the place up before I'm through."

+++++

Meanwhile, Rice, who had been watching Pete's apartment had followed them to the beauty shop and had watched the whole scene unfold. He called the chief and told him about another failed attempt and asked, "What do you want me to do now?"

The chief said, "It is just as well that your hit-man failed. I just received a cancellation of that contract. I'm not too upset about that. However, I don't care what you have to do, I want Pete Dover dead and I want it now." The chief closed his phone.

Rice knew he was in a dangerous spot. Pete was being protected. It was almost impossible to take him out. He knew he could be killed trying. However, he also knew that if he didn't do the deed, he would be killed by someone the chief hired. He knew there was nowhere to hide. He drove back to Pete's apartment and took a parking place where he could see Pete's parking place and the front door of his apartment. Rice was stressing out, trying to decide what action to take. He decided to take Pete out as soon as he got to his apartment. Rice didn't know why but it was about an hour later before Pete and Alice arrived.

Sam had followed Rice to the beauty shop and had watched the action, but was too far away to effect the situation. Now, he was back at Pete's apartment keeping an eye on Rice. He had the feeling that this was it. He believed Rice was about to try to take Pete out. He parked as close as possible to Rice and had a good view of him.

With his rifle across his lap, Rice watched as Pete and Alice got out of the car and started walking toward the apartment. "Damn," he thought. "Alice is between me and Pete." However, in spite of the problem, Rice was ready if a shot became available.

That happened when Alice and Pete turned the corner to walk to the apartment. Rice put the rifle barrel out the window and fired. However, just before he fired, Alice had gotten a glimpse of the weapon. She pushed Pete to the ground and fell on top of him.

Then, Sam fired twice. Rice's shot went over Pete and actually hit the apartment window. Both of Sam's bullets found their mark. The rifle fell to the ground. Rice slumped in his car seat.

Pete was alright, but still on the ground when he called the police. Alice and Sam made their way to Rice's car and found him dead. Both of Sam's shots had hit him. Alice yelled back to tell Pete he was dead. Everything seemed to be moving fast, as Pete called Sanders. "Sanders, it's over for now, Sam just killed Rice, and thank God he had been following him."

"I'll be right there," replied Sanders. Sanders, Gracie and Ruby had been on their way home and immediately turned around to go to Pete's apartment.

Chapter Twenty Seven

Helena
Coming Apart
July 8

    The headlines of the Helena and Memphis papers told the story of the suicide of a prominent farmer and citizen of Phillips County. "Leon Wesson took his own life," was the way the paper made the headline read. The article below the headline questioned what had happened to cause such a respected person to commit suicide. Mention was made that his son, Mike had been arrested for drug trafficking and was in the Shelby County jail.

    Joe Cole and Frank Castle were at the Big Island Restaurant eating breakfast and reading the paper, but mostly they were talking about their problems. They couldn't believe any of it. Just three days ago, they thought everything was working perfectly. First was the seizure of a load of marijuana and the arrest of Mike. Now, Wesson had committed suicide.

    They called the chief and since no one else was in the restaurant, they put the phone on speaker so all three could enter the conversation. Joe said, "Chief, what the hell is going on? We're sitting at the restaurant reading about Leon and can't figure out anything. What's your take on it?"

"I don't know for sure. Either Wesson couldn't handle the fact that his son had been arrested and was going to spend a lot of time in prison or he knew something that we don't know."

"What do you mean by that?" said Cole.

The chief replied, "I know he visited Mike in the county jail without anyone else being present. I also know that Pete Dover was with them part of the time. I don't know what was said, but if Dover offered Mike some kind of deal and he accepted, Wesson would have a hard time handling it. I also know that after talking with Mike, he tried to cancel the contract he had put out on Ruby."

"If Mike agreed to some kind deal, we're all in trouble. It may be time to close up shop and 'make it every man for himself'," responded Frank Castle.

"You may be right, but lets give it a few more days and see if we can put it back together," said the chief. "By the way, in case you haven't heard, my contractor was killed yesterday. One of his hit-men was also arrested. Pete Dover and Ruby Shipman are still alive."

When the chief had hung up the phone, Joe Cole said, "If it is the last thing I do, I'm going to get Ruby Shipman. She betrayed me and I'm going to bring her back here and made her pay. Just killing her is too easy for her. I want her to die very slowly and painfully."

"How you going to do that," asked Castle.

"I believe they will let their guard down now that the contractor has been killed and the hit-man arrested. They will feel much safer. I'm going to get some of the boys to go to Memphis and grab her and bring her back to the duck nest."

The duck nest was located on the Mississippi side of the river. It went out about one hundreds yards over the river and had not been used in years. Years ago it was used as a beer joint and dance hall.

+++++

Mike was sitting alone in his cell reading, for the second time, the letter from his dad when the guard came and said, "Wesson, you have a visitor. Follow me to the visitation room."

It was Ruby. She said, "Pete is in the building and will be here later. He wanted to let us have some private time."

Mike had not seen the newspaper and had not talked to anyone about his dad. His first words to Ruby was, "Ruby, did he really do it?"

"Yes, he jumped off the Helena Bridge late yesterday. Mike, I'm so sorry."

"Me too, but I want you to read his last word to me. I got this letter about an hour ago and it gives me so much peace to know he understood. Dad would have never been able to adjust to prison."

As Ruby read the letter, tears began to form in her eyes as she heard Leon Wesson call the child she was carrying his grandchild. Ruby reached across the table and held both of Mike's hands as they looked at each other with eyes filled with love.

"Mike, I love you so much. I do have one more thing to say about your dad. Homeland Security is listening in on the chief's calls and the last call your dad made to him was an effort to cancel the contract he had put out on me. So, while he didn't succeed, I know he tried and that means a lot to me."

"What do you mean, he didn't succeed?"

"A hit-man shot at me, but Sanders was able to block the shot with his car and he and Gracie arrested the woman."

"You could have been killed!"

"I owe Sanders and Gracie a lot."

"Me too," said Mike.

Just then, Pete entered the room, shook Mike's hand and sat down beside Ruby. "I sorry about your dad," he said.

"Thank you for your concern, but that is the way he wanted it and I just have to accept that."

"Mike, I know you asked your dad to tell you who the chief is. I don't know if he did or not."

Mike looked at Ruby who had read the letter and knew the answer. Ruby said nothing, so Mike said, "I know who the chief is, but I have one issue in our deal that I have a question about."

"What is it?" responded Pete.

"When I tell you everything I know, including the name of the chief, when do I get out of here?"

"We'll start working on your program as soon as I get the information. It shouldn't take long."

Mike looked at Ruby and asked, "What about the time between now and then?"

"It's usual for the person to remain in jail until in the program and location is worked out. That way they can go directly from jail to the witness protection program. That's much safer."

"I understand that, but I also understand that Ruby could have been killed yesterday. Needless to say, I don't want that. I want to be out of here so I can help protect her."

"Mike I know how you feel, but I don't know if I can work it out. You'll have to give me some time. I have to talk to Witcher before I make you any promises."

Again, Mike looked at Ruby and then he said, "Then you'll have to give me some time before I give you all the information that you want. This includes the name of the chief."

+++++

Pete had dropped Ruby off at Sanders and Gracie's before he went to his apartment for lunch with Alice. Ruby was feeling some guilt because she had been loyal to Mike and had not told Pete who the chief was. This really wasn't like her. She had always put job first, but now everything was different. She was in love with Mike and was carrying his child. They were going to be married.

When Alice met Pete at the door, she said, "Don't ever do that again! I can't handle it."

"Don't do what again?"

Don't go off by yourself and leave me here to worry about you! It's my job to protect you and I can't do that if I'm not with you."

"Gripe, gripe, gripe---is this the way it's going to be after we're married?" Pete teased. Pete had made the decision to ask Alice to marry him some time ago and had even bought the ring; however, he didn't mean to do it like this. He wanted to be romantic and maybe even get down on one knee.

Alice was still pretty angry when she said, "I didn't know we were getting married. When did you make that decision? Most women, that I know, would like to be asked before the man assumes she wants to marry him."

"I'm sorry if I took you for granted. I really meant to ask the question in a romantic way. Will this make it okay?" Pete got down on one knee and said, "Alice, I would like for you to be my wife. Would you marry me and wear my ring forever?" With that he produced the ring from his pocket.

All the anger in Alice melted away. She looked at the ring in his hand. It was the most beautiful ring she had ever seen. Then, she held out her left hand for him to place it on her finger. There were tears in her eyes as she threw her arms around the man she loved. She knew they would fight; it was part of their DNA. As Pete carried her to his bedroom to confirm the commitment they had just made, she learned "make-up sex was the best."

+++++

The key leaders of the drug ring, which included, Frank Castle, Joe Cole, Roger Sneed and Bob Wilkins, were gathered in the chief's office. The news was not good. It seemed the Justice Department had gathered enough evidence to arrest them all, except maybe the chief.

To the best of his knowledge, the FED still did not know who the leader of the drug trafficking ring was and the chief wanted to keep it that way. As far as he knew, the four men in front of him were the only ones who knew he was the chief. Rice had known but he was dead. Wesson had known, too, but he had killed himself.

The chief had considered taking care of the loose ends by killing the four men, but had decided to find another way to keep them quiet. He said, "I'm afraid it's over. The FED is closing in and unless you can hide, all of you are likely to be arrested. You have all made a lot of money, but you're going to need a lot of money to fight this in court and if you're found guilty, you're going to need a lot of money when you get out of prison."

"I'm going to be totally honest; I am prepared to give each of you twenty five million dollars. I want to pay you to forget you ever knew me."

"Is it that bad?" asked Sneed.

"Yes, I believe it is."

"When do we get our money?" asked Wilkins.

"Today, I have deposited your money in several different banks throughout the world. They are banks I've used in our business, so you can trust them. The deposit slips are in the envelopes in front of you."

"Chief, what do you plan to do?"

"I'm closing down everything I can as quick as I can, and then I'm leaving for parts unknown to anyone but me. I would advise you to do the same."

+++++

Pete had gotten an okay from Witcher to release Mike into Ruby's custody as soon as he got all the information he needed. Mike had already confirmed everything Pete had. Pete really only needed the name of the chief. It was time to go back to the jail and get that information, so he called Ruby to ask her to go with him.

The two of them were sitting at the same table facing Mike and after some small talk, Pete said, "I got the approval from Witcher with one minor exception. You can be released as soon as I get the chief's name."

"That's what I want, but what's the exception?"

Pete had not told Ruby the exception and she was startled when Pete said, "You can leave the jail, but you will be released into Ruby's custody."

"Since I have agreed to be in her control for the rest of my life, it might as well begin now," replied Mike. "So what's the process of getting it done?"

At that moment, Ruby loved him even more than she had before.

"Give me the name and I will clear it with the jailer and we'll walk out of here together."

Mike handed Pete the letter from his dad and said, "I want you to read the letter and know that the information you need came from my Dad."

Pete scanned the letter until he got to the part that said, "P.S. The chief of the drug ring is Robert Shelby who owns a chain of Supermarkets." After reading the letter a second time, he asked Mike if he could make a copy of the letter. Mike agreed and Pete left Ruby and Mike alone in the visitation room while he got the copy made and asked the jailer to release Mike into Ruby's custody.

With the business completed, Pete went back to the visitation room, asked the guard to unlock the door and the three of them walked out of the jail. On the way to the car, Pete called Witcher to let her know what was going on and to ask her to get one hundred agents to meet at the Department of Justice building at 4:00 a.m. tomorrow prepared to complete Operation Delta Pride.

+++++

Ruby had already talked with Gracie about Mike staying with them until they could figure out something else. Gracie had agreed, so Pete dropped them off at Gracie and Sanders' home. Pete was in a hurry to get home and see Alice. They had just finished making love when the call came for him to come to the jail to see Mike. Pete was anxious to get back to Alice and talk about their future together.

They had a lot of decisions to make. "Was Alice planning to stay with the FBI? Where would they live? Did Pete plan to continue to work for the Department of Justice? If they planned to have children, when and how many?" All these questions and many others filled Pete's mind as he drove home to see Alice.

Alice saw Pete as he parked his car in the drive, so when he opened the door to the apartment, she was standing there with nothing on but a smile and said, "You left before you finished your job."

When he saw her and heard her teasing him, he forgot all the things he wanted to talk about. He just wanted her.

+++++

There was no doubt, Joe Cole was afraid of what was about to happen. He believed the chief and had decided to get out of town as soon as possible. His biggest regret was the fact that he didn't have the time to take care of Ruby. However, it may take years but he was going to get that bitch and she would know that it came from him. No one was going to use sex to pump him for information and get away with it.

However, now was not the time, because Cole needed to get his ticket out of the country. He was lucky in that he had made some plans. He had identification in the name of George Freeman. He also had a credit card in that name.

Calling a travel agency, he asked them to get him a ticket for a trip to Bogota, Colombia. He said, "I want to leave tomorrow and the earlier in the day the better."

Cole had been to Bogota two years ago and set up an account with the Bank of Bogota. He called the bank to make sure his account was in order and told them there would be money coming from the US in the name of Joe Cole. After completing the information with the bank, Cole called his local bank and told them to transfer the $100,000 in his saving account to the bank in Bogota. He knew he would need additional cash for spending money, but that he could pick that up at his bank in Memphis tomorrow when he was catching the plane.

The travel agency returned Cole's call to say his flight would leave gate seven at the Memphis airport at 8:00 in the morning.

In the meantime, Shelby was making the same kind of plans. He already had his money issues taken care of and was finishing up with a plane ticket to the Caribbean Island of Aruba. He had yet to decide where he would go from there.

When Shelby's phone rang, it was the travel agency with information about his ticket. His plane would leave from Memphis tomorrow from gate seventeen, at 7:30 a.m. and he would have one lay-over.

Chapter Twenty Eight

Memphis—Helena
The Round-Up
July 9

    It was 4:00 in the morning and over one hundred agents had gathered at the Department of Justice building in Memphis. Debra Witcher was there, but there was no doubt that Pete Dover was in charge of the operation known as Operation Delta Pride. Today was the day that all the hard work was going to pay off.

    The round-up would include everyone involved in the drug trafficking in Helena including the higher leadership like Joe Cole and Frank Castle, who were thought to be leading citizens of Phillips County. It would include the airport baggage people and those at the warehouse on Brooks Road. The classmates from Sneed, Weeks and King were on the list of those to be arrested as well. Robert Shelby, the chief, was at the top of that list.

    Pete even had FBI agents in Chicago to arrest those who had received the stolen goods and the drugs that were shipped by trucks from Helena and Memphis. There were also agents in Little Rock and Fayetteville to make the arrest of the people who were in those warehouses to pay for and unload the drugs.

Pete wanted to arrest Robert Shelby himself. He wanted to be the one to look him in the face and tell him that he and his whole organization were going down. He wanted to say to him, "You tried to have me killed on three different times and failed. Now I'm the one that's going to put you away." It was fitting that Alice was going with him to arrest Shelby.

What was true for Pete concerning Shelby was also true for Ruby. She wanted Joe Cole bad. Pete had tried to talk her into staying at the Department of Justice building and help as other agents brought in the people they were arresting, but she was having none of that. She was determined to go after Cole. Of course, there was no way Mike was going to let her go without him. Another agent was assigned to Ruby and the three of them went to Helena to arrest Joe Cole and Frank Castle.

By 6:00 a.m., everybody had their assignments. They knew exactly where they were going and who they were going to arrest. A total of two hundred thirteen people were to be arrested and brought back to Memphis. It was going to be a great day for those trying to slow down the trafficking of drugs in the US. Pete said a silent prayer before he sent everyone off to do their job.

+++++

When Pete and Alice got to Robert Shelby's home, they found the house was dark and there was no activity. Everything seemed deserted. They knew that Shelby's wife had left him six months ago and that Shelby now lived alone. Pete rang the door bell once, then twice and finally a third time. They got no response.

They were armed with a search warrant, so when no one answered, they broke the lock on the door and entered the house. They found the house was completely empty. Items were left scattered all over the bedroom to reveal that someone had packed in a hurry. Papers on the desk in the den told the story of Shelby planning to board a plane to Aruba. The plane was set to take off at 7:30 a.m. The interesting thing was the name of the person flying was Richard Maxwell.

It took a while, but Pete figured that Robert Shelby was flying to Aruba under the false name of Richard Maxwell. Pete looked at his watch and found it was just after 7:00 a.m. He didn't have time to get to the airport before 7:30 a.m.

"What are we going to do?" asked Alice. "They will never get the plane stopped in time."

"I have an idea." Pete dialed Al's number in air traffic control. When he got Al on the phone he said, "Al, you have a plane leaving the airport at 7:30 going to Aruba."

"Do you know the flight number?" asked Al.

Alice moved some of the papers around and said, "Here it is. The flight is American Airlines 3544 leaving from gate seventeen."

Al said, "I heard that. American Airlines 3544 is about five minutes from take off."

"Al, this is important. Can you stop the plane?" Pete asked.

"Why?"

"Because the top man of the drug ring is on that plane," responded Pete.

"No problem, I'll get it done. We'll say the plane is being delayed because of engine problems. I'll have security circle the plane. How quick can you be here?"

"Thirty minutes and thanks a lot."

+++++

The pilot of flight 3544 made the announcement that the plane was having engine problems and would return to gate seventeen so the engine could be repaired. The pilot asked everyone to be patience and remain seated. He said, "The problem should be taken care of in short order and then we'll be on our way."

Shelby wondered what was going on. It was probably just as the pilot had said, but the suspicious side of him was nervous that it could be about him. In his mind, he went through all the preparation he had done. "Had he done or said anything that would give his plan to the leave the country away?" he asked himself. Then, he knew. If the Feds had been in his house, they could have found notes that concerned his flight plans. He had meant to clean that up before he left, but knew in his heart that he had left them on his desk in the den.

Looking around, Shelby found there is no where to hide on a plane. The flight attendants were doing their job. They seemed to be everywhere taking care of the needs of the passengers. It seemed there were more security people than normal. Then, he saw him, and he was no flight attendant or security personnel. The man looking him in the eye and walking toward him was Pete Dover and there was absolutely nothing he could do.

"Robert Shelby, you're under arrest for your involvement in money laundering and drug trafficking," said Pete.

"But my name is Richard Maxwell. You have the wrong man," shouted Shelby.

After the cuffs were put on his hands and he was read his rights, Pete said, "Shelby, we're not playing games like that. We know who you are. Now, let go."

+++++

As Pete led Shelby off the plane, his phone rang. It was Ruby and she said, "We have Frank Castle in custody. However, we are at Joe Cole's home and he is not here. His wife says he left for Memphis last night. She thinks he has a meeting at Sneed, Weeks and King today."

"We just found Shelby on a plane trying to leave the country. It may be that Cole is trying to do the same. Use the search warrant and look for anything that might help us locate him. Meanwhile I'll keep my eyes open for him here."

"Will do and if I find anything I'll give you a call," replied Ruby.

Pete came off the plane at gate seventeen and started walking toward the exit of the airport. As he walked, he looked for Joe Cole just in case he was trying to board a plane. As luck would have it, when he got to gate seven he saw Cole standing in line waiting to board the plane. As yet, Cole had not seen him, so Pete called security and asked them to meet him at gate eight.

When four airport security people arrived, Pete told them the situation. He asked one to stay with Alice, who was guarding Shelby, and the other three to go with him to gate seven to make sure that Cole didn't escape.

Cole had no idea he was being watched, which allowed Pete to walk right up to him, tap him on the shoulder and say, "Joe Cole, you're under arrest." Cole turned to run, but ran right into a security person who wrestled him to the floor.

Cuffs were placed on his hands and his rights were read to him. With the help of the security people, both men were led to and put in Pete's car. Pete called Ruby to let her know that Cole was in custody, thanked security for their help, got in his car and drove off. "Thank God, this part of the operation is over," he said to Alice.

+++++

It was 4:00 in the afternoon before all the agents had returned to the Department of Justice building. Operation Delta Pride had been very successful. Of the two hundred thirteen warrants, the agents had arrested two hundred five people. They had missed eight people but felt sure they would still find them. All the leadership was in jail. The mood was that of celebration.

Debra Witcher found Pete and Alice and told them what a wonderful job they had done. Then she noticed the ring on Alice's finger. "Congratulation on your engagement. Who is the lucky groom?" she said.

Alice replied, "I've been with Pete, night and day for weeks and somehow I fell in love with him. We will plan our wedding as soon as this circus is over."

Mike and Ruby joined the threesome and heard them talking about marriage. Ruby said, "Debra, add Mike and I to the list of people who fell in love during Operation Delta Pride. We will be married before you send us to the witness protection program."

"Then you better do it soon, because you're leaving in two days."

Mike looked at Ruby and said, "Honey, I'm ready. Can we do it at noon tomorrow?"

"We can, but let me get with Gracie and let her help me plan it. At the very least, I have to have a new dress and my hair fixed. It may even be possible to put together a beautiful garden wedding in their backyard if they don't mind."

Al and Sally had been invited to the celebration because of the part they had in Operation Delta Pride and especially because Al had stopped the plane that Robert Shelby intended to leave the country on. Sally too, was wearing a ring on her left hand. She said, "Three couples met and fell in love during Operation Delta Pride. It was wonderful getting to know everyone but especially Al. I look forward to at least one hundred years with him."

"Romance is in the air. Maybe if I would get out in the field more, I would meet someone and fall in love," said Debra as she walked away. Right now all was right with the world and Debra Witcher was proud to be a part of making that happen.

Chapter Twenty Nine

Memphis
Epilogue
December 25

    Next week, they would be leaving for Gulf Shores and would spend the next three months there visiting with their friends Joe and Amy Appleton. They had met the Appleton's at Tunica right after Stan had won the 145 million dollars in a Power Ball Lottery. Their friendship had grown over the years.
    Stan was feeling much better these days, but after Stan's heart problems in July, they had sold the motor home. This would be their first big trip traveling in the car and staying in the condo that had been purchased by the Dover family.
    While they were gone, the children would be moving their stuff to St Bernards Village, in their hometown of Jonesboro, Arkansas. They had bought a house there, because it provided the increasing personal care they needed in their old age. When they could no longer live in their own home, they would move to the assisted living portion and then later the nursing home.
    Pat looked around at her family gathered in their old house in Jonesboro for the last time. Over the years she had seen a lot of changes. Her mind went on one of those "precious

memories" tours that happen to people when they are in the 80's.

The tour begins when she found out Stan had won the money and she learned he had slept with another woman. She had long since forgiven him, but there were still times when she remembered. With blackmail and murders to be solved, that year had been rocky for their marriage and their family, but they had survived it and their family had grown stronger. Their children, Andy, Gracie, and Sam had become strong, mature adults, as they formed the detective agency which had done very well.

As Pat surveyed the room, her eyes fell on her granddaughter Susan and her family. She enjoyed a wonderful husband and three children, two boys and a girl. Susan's life after college had also had a rocky start. The murder of her college boyfriend and her kidnapping, when they were in New Orleans, was a terrible ordeal. However, even in all that pain, there was a happy ending. That's when she met Dan. He was a doctor who had been running away from life when Susan was having a hard time finding herself, but together they had become a wonderful family filled with hope, joy and love.

A crying baby reminded Pat that this last year had seen the most change in the family. It had grown. There was Susan and Dan's new baby, Shane, who was ignoring the fact that his parents had told him he was to be seen and not heard.

New to the family was Sally, Al's wife. Sally often said, "I had to crash my plane to get Al to propose to me." Pat guessed that must be right, because it was less than an hour after the crash that he asked her to join the family. Both of them were still working with the airlines.

Also new to the family was Alice, Pete's wife. Alice had resigned from the FBI and joined the detective agency.

Pete was still at the Department of Justice and was working on some new case that he wouldn't or couldn't talk about. Pat had heard that they fought a lot and that they believed make-up sex was the best. She thought, "It must be true for them, they are expecting twins in April."

Pat was looking forward to the trip to Gulf Shores, but mostly, she was looking forward to coming home to their new house. She wanted to sit in her new recliner, put her feet up and "enjoy the memories" and maybe, if she and Stan were lucky, they would get to make a few new memories.

Want More

J Maxwell West

Please continue reading for a

Bonus excerpt

From

For the Love of Money

ISBN13 Number
9781468014785
Available from
west4937@sbcglobal.net
jpbooks.net
amazon.com

CHAPTER ONE

Stan was awake again. It was 3:00 a.m. Sherry, a late "thirty something" year old Stan had picked up at the Casino, was asleep beside him. They had been playing Blackjack at the same table. After an hour or so of flirting she had invited him to her condo which she said was nearby. Stan followed her 2009 silver SUV and sure enough about 2 miles later she turned into Tunica National Subdivision and stopped in front of a condo that had the number 198 on the front door. He pulled his 2008, F150 Ford red pickup in beside her. It had been one hell of a night. Of course, Stan wound up in bed with this woman who was built for what he had in mind. And she knew how to use everything that the good Lord had given her. But now he was awake and his mind would not shut down.

Getting out of bed he found his pants, which were hanging on the closet door where he had left them. Making sure his billfold was still there, he put them on as he started toward the kitchen. He needed coffee. Finding the "Mr. Coffee" was easy but now where would he find the filters and coffee. Finally, as he opened the last cabinet door, he found them. After putting the water, filter and coffee in the Mr. Coffee, Stan sat down at the table to give it time to perk and him time to think.

He reached for his billfold, opened it and took out a folded piece of paper. As Stan unfolded the paper, a power-ball ticket dropped to the table. The ticket was for May 15, 2010 and the numbers on the ticket were: 15-21-23-28-36 and the power-ball number was 20. Checking the newspaper clipping he had carefully cut out and folded, Stan first compared the numbers: 15-21-23-28-36 & 20. He had the winning number and after six days he still could not believe it. He had not told a soul.

Stan felt like the young boy who finally got a girl to say "yes". Stan heard himself say, "Now that I've got it---what am I going to do with it?" Taking a pen from his pocket and finding something to write on he looked again at the newspaper clipping. Grand prize $145 million or, if he took the cash, $72.1 million. If he took the cash, the government would take out 35%. Stan wrote down $72,000,000 times 35% equals $25,235,000 for the government. That leaves $46,865,000 for Stan Dover. "What am I going to do with it?" Stan carefully placed the ticket in the paper, folded it and placed it back in his billfold which he placed in his left back pocket of his jeans.

As he poured himself a cup of coffee, he remembered all the things he had read on the internet during the past six days about lottery winners. Much good had been done by people who had won. Families had become millionaires because Uncle Joe had won the jackpot. Stan read about Andrew Jackson "Jack" Whittaker Jr., a West Virginia businessman who won $315 million on December 25, 2002 in the Powerball Lottery. Jack give 10% of his winnings to a Christian charity, gave the woman that sold him the winning ticket a house and car, and set up a charity that provides food and clothing to the needy. However, Jack Whittaker died broke.

Strangely enough, winning millions has been the worst thing to happen to many people. Alex and Rhonda Toth won 13 million in the Florida Lottery. Eighteen years later Alex was dead and Rhonda was in jail for tax fraud. The 13 million was long gone because of their lavish lifestyle and gambling debt. Billie Bob Harrell won 31 million in the Texas lottery in 1997. Because he could not say "no", people took advantage of him, his marriage crumbled as his bank account dwindled. Sadly, Billie Bob couldn't handle the pressure of his new life and blew his brains out with a shotgun within two years after winning.

Setting his cup in the sink, Stan decided he needed to finish getting dressed and get on the road. He would need to face the music and he may as well get started. Pat, his wife, would be worried about him. Pat and Stan had been married 51 years and this was the first time he had been unfaithful. "Damn, now I have two problems." He heard himself say: "What do I do about the money? And what do I tell Pat about last night?"

During the two hour drive from Tunica, MS, which is the third-largest gaming region in the U.S., to Jonesboro, AR, a college town of 60,000 in northeast Arkansas, Stan made two decisions. He would tell Pat about the Powerball Jackpot. After all, she was the money brains in the family and he needed her help deciding how to handle the money. But, he would lie about last night. He would tell her he played blackjack until about 1:00 am and was sleepy when he got in the truck and leaned back to take a short nap. When he woke up it was 5 a.m.

It was 7:30 a.m. as he turned into the driveway of his house at 4005 Parkview. The house was one of those small two bedroom/one bath frame houses that were built right after World War II. Stan had lived in the house (off and on) since 1956. About thirty years ago he had added another bedroom and bath to the house. He and Pat were comfortable here. They had raised their three kids here. Since his retirement as a real estate broker, two years ago, he had been working on Pat's "honey-do" list and was making some headway. The old place was looking pretty good. Stan noticed the lights were on.

Opening the front door, Stan yells out, "Honey, I'm home."

"Well, it's about time," shouted Pat from the kitchen.

As Stan walked into the kitchen, he could feel the tension that had filled the room. Pat was mad as hell and he was about to get it. She poured two cups of coffee and set them on the table. She looked through Stan and said, "Set down, we need to talk, now!" As they sat down Stan did not know what to expect but he feared life as he had known it for 51 years had come to an end. Was all this about last night? Did she know what he had done?

Looking Stan straight in the eye, Pat said, "I need to know what's going on with you. Now!"

Giving her that look that he had developed over the years, he said, "I don't know what you mean."

"Don't give me that shit. For the past six days you have been a different person. You don't talk to me. You're never here and when you are, there is a distant look in your eyes. To top it off you laid out all night. In our 51 years you have never done that. I need some answers."

"You knew I was going to Tunica to play blackjack. I was winning a little and it got late before I knew it. I cashed out and went to the truck about 1:00 a.m. To tell you the truth, I was sleepy and leaned back to take a short nap. It was 5:00 a.m. before I woke up."

"I don't believe you, but even if I did, what about the last six days? You have just not been the person I married and have lived with all these years. What in the hell is going on?"

Stan decided this was the time to tell Pat about the Powerball Jackpot. He reached across the table with his right hand and took her hand. With his left hand, he reached for his billfold. Stan looked at his loving wife of 51 years and said, "Honey, I have something to show you." Opening his billfold, he took out the newspaper clipping. As he was unfolding the clipping, the Powerball ticket fell out.

Reaching for the ticket, Pat asked, "What the hell is this?"

Handing Pat the newspaper clipping Stan said, "Read this." Stan leaned back and watched Pat as she read the clipping.

"So, the Jackpot is $145 million. What does that have to do with anything?"

"Look at numbers on the ticket and compare it to the newspaper"

Stan watched as Pat read aloud the numbers off the newspaper: "15-21-23-28-36 & 20". Then she picked up the ticket: "15-21-23-28-36 & 20". Pat couldn't speak. She looked dumb-founded. After what seemed like five minutes, Pat asked, "Is this your ticket?"

In the most loving voice Stan could use, he responded with, "It is our ticket and I need your help in knowing what to do with all this."

Pat could not believe this was happening. They had won the Powerball Jackpot of 145 million dollars. They had always had to watch their money to have enough to raise their three children. For the past two years, with Stan's retirement pension and the kids on their own, they had enjoyed a little breathing room. But 145 million dollars would mean major changes in their life. Now Pat understood what had been going on in Stan's life for the past six days. With this news and the excitement that it came with it, she totally forgot about Stan staying out all night. Pat asked, "What are we going to do with all that money?"

Excerpts from Chapter Three

It was 6:15 p.m. when they got to LuckyStrike. Pat still had $600 of her $750 and Stan had $700. They went by the Diner and got a bite to eat and then went on to play. Stan noticed that Tony was dealing at the table where he liked to play. Stan enjoyed playing when Tony was dealing. He had been playing about two hours when Sherry sat down in an empty chair beside him.

"I don't know if I ever sat next to a millionaire before" Sherry said letting Stan know she did indeed know about the Powerball Jackpot.

"What do you mean?" responded Stan.

"You know what I mean" answered Sherry, "I saw you and your wife on TV and learned you won $145 million in a Powerball Jackpot."

"Actually, I only cleared about $40 million of that since I took the cash and paid the taxes." Stan knew his goose was cooked. It was just a matter of how much she wanted. He had $1000 in his "rat-hole" that he might give her if that would end it. But his thinking was, this can't go on and on.

Looking as sexy as possible, she asked, "When do I get my part?"

"What do you mean your part?" Stan could tell that did not go over good with Sherry so he added, "I have $1000 that I can give you today if that will end this thing. I have already given you $500 and I think $1500 is enough for a piece of ass." Maybe he shouldn't have put it just that way.

Sherry wasn't looking sexy any longer. In fact she looked about as mean as the devil herself as she faced Stan. "I want $1 million or I will tell your wife and show her pictures of our night together and you had better make up your mind in a hurry because I think I see her coming toward us."

Stan turned and sure enough Pat had seen them playing and talking together and was walking toward them. There would already be hell to pay because Pat had told Stan she did not trust that woman and he should avoid her. Stan said, "We locked that money up in long term investments and I can't get to that much money. I can give you $1000 today and I will have to get back to you about any additional money?"

Just before Pat get to the table Sherry said, "I'll take the $1,000 today and you better believe there will be more, about $1 million more."

As Pat got to the table she said, "Stan, honey, introduce me to your friend. Haven't I seen you playing with her before?"

"Pat, this is Sherry. She plays blackjack about as often as I do and we run into each other from time to time."

Pat asked, "Sherry, what is your last name and where do you live?"

"My name is Sherry Wolf and I live about two miles from here in a condo. Your husband is a good player and I am trying to pick his brain so I can learn to play better. He's helped me quite a bit. In fact I am up about $1500 because of him."

"Just make sure that is all he helps you with," Pat said as she turned and walked away.

After a minute, Sherry gave Stan an envelope and said, "Give me the $1000 now and I will give you two weeks to get the million together. By the way there are some pictures in that envelope you need to look at." Then she took the money and got up from table and left the Casino.

Stan took a bathroom break to look in the envelope. He found three pictures of Sherry and him in various sex acts along with a DVD. He could only imagine what was on the DVD. He didn't understand any of this. It had to mean someone else was in the condo with them taking the pictures and running the video camera. It meant Sherry set him up.

~~~~~~~

Stan was knocking on the door of condo #198 on Magnolia Dr, just two miles from LuckyStrike. Sherry answered the door, invited him in and said, "Did you bring my money?"

"Not today", said Stan, "you said I had two weeks and besides that I can't figure out any way to get that kind of money out of the investment account without Pat knowing about it."

"Well, if you don't get it in 12 days, she will know it because I will tell her myself. After all, I know you live at 4005 Parkview in Jonesboro, Arkansas. I would not hesitate to drive up there and tell her straight out." This argument continued for about an hour and a half and got rather loud. When Stan left, nothing had been settled but he was sure she would drive to Jonesboro and tell Pat about that unfaithful night if he did not come up with $1 million in twelve days.

~~~~~~

The TV was on and the news was reporting there had been a murder in Tunica, MS. The reporter said, "The body of Sherry Wolf was found at 9:48 pm last night in her apartment at 198 Magnolia Dr. She had been shot. No other details are available at this time." A picture of Sherry was shown on the TV.

"Hey, isn't that your girlfriend?" asked Pat.

"She was not my girlfriend but it does look like the person I had been trying to teach to play blackjack. I never knew her last name until she introduced herself to you the other night." Stan did not know what he was feeling. A person he had known, in the Biblical sense, had been murdered and he felt bad about that. However, this ended the blackmail threat. He didn't have to worry about the $1 million. In fact, he did not have anything to worry about. He and Pat could get on with their life. They could buy the RV and begin their travels and Pat could begin to look for a new place to live. Life was good again.

CHAPTER FOUR

At 9:15 a.m. Monday, September 13, the doorbell ring and Stan went to the door. Two men were standing there and introduced themselves as Scot Long and Mark Brown. Producing their badges Scot Long said, "We are both detectives for the Tunica County Sheriff's Department. May we come in?" As soon as they walked into the living room Detective Long asked, "Are you Stan Dover?"